Monsieur Ibrahim
and the Flowers of the Koran

&

Oscar and the Lady in Pink

Monsieur Ibrahim
and the Flowers of the Koran

&

Oscar and the Lady in Pink

Eric-Emmanuel Schmitt
Translated by Marjolijn de Jager

Other Press • New York

Originally published as *Monsieur Ibrahim et les Fleurs du Coran* and *Oscar et la Dame Rose*. Copyright © 2001, 2002, respectfully, Èditions Albin Michel S.A.

Translation copyright © 2003 Other Press

Production Editor: Robert D. Hack

This book was set in 10.5 pt. Sabon by Alpha Graphics of Pittsfield, New Hampshire.

10 9 8 7 6 5 4 3 2 1

Library of Congress Cataloging-in-Publication Data

ISBN 1-59051-091-7

CIP data is available from the Library of Congress.

Monsieur Ibrahim
and the Flowers of the Koran

&

Oscar and the Lady in Pink

Monsieur Ibrahim
and the Flowers of the Koran

For Bruno Abraham-Kremer

WHEN I WAS ELEVEN years old I broke open my piggy bank and went to see the whores.

My piggy bank was made of glazed porcelain, the color of vomit, with a slit that allowed you to put coins in but not to take them out. My father had chosen it, this one-way piggy bank, because it matched his outlook on life—money is made to be saved, not spent.

There were two hundred francs inside the pig's belly. Four months of work.

One morning, before I left for school, my father said:

"Moses, I don't understand. . . . There's money missing. . . . From now on, when you do the shopping I want you to write down everything you spend in the kitchen ledger."

So it wasn't enough that I was being yelled at both in school and at home, that I had to clean, study, cook, do the groceries. It wasn't enough that I was living alone in a large, dark apartment that was empty and loveless, that I was a slave rather than the son of a lawyer who did not have much business anymore and no wife. I now had to be treated like a thief as well! Since he already suspected me of stealing, I might as well just do it.

So there were two hundred francs inside the piggy bank. Two hundred francs—that's what a girl cost in the Rue de Paradis. It was the price of becoming a man.

The first few asked me for my identity card. In spite of my voice and my size—I was as big as a horse—they seemed to doubt that I was sixteen, although that is what I told them. They must have seen me walk by and grow up over these past years, hooked onto my shopping bag full of vegetables.

At the end of the street beneath an overhang stood a new one. She was plump and pretty as a picture. I showed her my money. She smiled.

"You're sixteen, are you?"

"Sure, since this morning."

We went upstairs. I could barely believe it, she was twenty-two, she was old, and she was all mine. She showed me how to wash and then how to make love.

Obviously, I already knew, but I let her tell me anyway so she'd be more at ease, and besides I liked her voice, which was a little sullen, a little sad. The whole time, I was on the point of fainting. When we were done, she gently caressed my hair and said:

"You should come back and bring me a little present."

That almost ruined my pleasure—I had forgotten the little present. There it was, I was a man, I'd had my baptism between the thighs of a woman, I could barely stand up because my legs were still shaking, and already the trouble had begun—I'd forgotten the famous little present.

I ran back to the apartment, dashed into my room, looked around to see what I might give her that was most cherished, then ran back double speed to the Rue de Paradis. The girl was beneath the overhang again. I gave her my stuffed bear.

It was just about then that I met Monsieur Ibrahim.

Monsieur Ibrahim had always been old. In the memory of everyone in the Rue Bleue and the Rue du Faubourg-Poissonnière, it was agreed that, from eight o'clock in the morning until the middle of the night, they had always seen Monsieur Ibrahim in his grocery store squashed between his cash register and the cleaning products, one leg in the aisle and the other under the boxes of matches, a gray work shirt over a white dress shirt, ivory teeth beneath an austere mustache, and pistachio-colored eyes—green and brown—lighter than his dark skin that bore the stains of wisdom.

For it was the general opinion that Monsieur Ibrahim was a sage. Probably because for at least forty years he had been the only Arab in a Jewish street. Probably because he smiled a lot and said little. Probably because he seemed untouched by the usual commotion of ordinary mortals, particularly Parisian mortals, never moving, like a branch grafted onto his stool, never clearing his stall for anyone to see, and vanishing between midnight and eight in the morning to nobody knew where.

So I did the shopping and made the meals every day. I bought only canned food. If I went to buy it daily, it wasn't so it'd be fresh, no, but because my father would leave me money for just one day at a time, and, besides, it was easier to cook that way!

When I began to steal from my father to punish him for having suspected me, I also started to steal from Monsieur Ibrahim. I was somewhat ashamed but, in order to struggle against my shame, I would think very hard when I paid him:

After all, he's only an Arab!

Every day I'd stare Monsieur Ibrahim straight in the eyes and that would give me courage.

After all, he's only an Arab.

"I'm not an Arab, Momo. I'm from the Golden Crescent."

I collected my groceries and went out into the street, stunned. Monsieur Ibrahim had heard me think! So, if he could hear me think, he knew that I was ripping him off, too, perhaps?

The next day, I didn't swipe a single can but asked him:

"What is that, the Golden Crescent?"

I have to admit that all night long I had imagined Monsieur Ibrahim sitting on the point of a golden crescent flying through a starry sky.

"It's a region that goes from Anatolia to Persia, Momo."

The following day, as I took out my wallet, I added:

"My name is not Momo but Moses."

The day after that it was he who added:

"I know your name is Moses, that's exactly why I call you Momo. It's less grand."

The following day, as I was counting out my change, I asked:

"What does it matter to you? Moses is Jewish, not Arabic."

"I'm not an Arab, Momo. I'm a Muslim."

"So then why do they say you're this street's only Arab if you're not an Arab?"

"In the grocery business, Momo, Arab means 'open from eight in the morning until midnight and even on Sundays.'"

That's how the conversation went. One sentence a day. We had plenty of time. He, because he was old, and I, because I was young. And every other day I'd steal a can of food.

It would have taken us a year or two, I think, to have a one-hour conversation had we not met Brigitte Bardot.

Great excitement in the Rue Bleue. Traffic stopped. The street was closed off. They were shooting a film.

Anyone with a sex drive in the Rue Bleue, the Rue Papillon, and the Faubourg-Poissonnière was on the alert. Women wanted to check and see if she was as fine as they said; men weren't thinking at all, whatever they might have to say was stuck in their fly. Brigitte Bardot is here! Wow, Brigitte Bardot in the flesh!

Me, I sat down at the window. I looked at her and she made me think of the neighbors' cat on the fourth floor, a pretty little female cat who loves stretching in the sun on the balcony and seems to live, breathe, and wink only to arouse admiration. Looking more closely, I also discovered that she really resembled the whores of Rue de Paradis without being aware that, actually, the whores of the Rue de Paradis disguised themselves as Brigitte Bardot to attract customers. Finally, to my utter amazement, I notice that Monsieur Ibrahim is standing in his doorway. It is the first time—at least since I've been alive—that he left his stool.

Having watched the little Bardot creature flutter her wings in front of the cameras, I start thinking about the lovely blonde who owns my bear and I decide to go down to Monsieur Ibrahim's and take advantage of his inattention to snatch a few cans of food. Disaster! He's gone back to sit behind his cash register. His eyes are smiling above the soaps and clothespins as he watches Bardot. I've never seen him like this.

"Are you married, Monsieur Ibrahim?"

"Yes, of course I'm married."

He isn't used to being asked any questions.

At that moment I could have sworn he wasn't as old as everybody thought.

"Monsieur Ibrahim! Imagine you're on a boat with your wife and Brigitte Bardot. Your boat is sinking. What do you do?"

"I bet my wife knows how to swim."

I've never seen his eyes laugh like that. They're laughing uproariously, they're making a huge racket, those eyes.

Suddenly, action stations! Monsieur Ibrahim is standing at attention—Brigitte Bardot enters the grocery store!

"Good morning, Monsieur, would you have any water?"

"Of course, Miss."

And then the unimaginable happens—Monsieur Ibrahim himself goes to get a bottle of water from a shelf and brings it to her.

"Thank you, sir. How much do I owe you?"

"Forty francs, Miss."

Brigitte gives a start. Me too. A bottle of water was worth about two francs at the time, not forty.

"I had no idea that water was so rare here."

"It's not the water that is rare, Miss. It's real stars."

He said it so charmingly, with such an irresistible smile, that Brigitte Bardot blushed a little, took out her forty francs, and went away.

I couldn't get over it.

"Really, Monsieur Ibrahim, you have some nerve."

"Well now, my little Momo, I have to find some way to pay myself back for all the cans you've been swiping from me, don't I?"

That was the day we became friends.

It's true that from then on I could have gone elsewhere to steal my cans, but Monsieur Ibrahim made me swear that I wouldn't do that:

"Momo, if you must go on stealing, do it here, from me."

Besides, during the days that followed Monsieur Ibrahim gave me lots of hints on how to extract money from my father without his realizing it. Serving him bread, a day or two old, and putting it in the oven first; gradually adding more and more chicory to the coffee; reusing tea bags; mixing his usual Beaujolais with wine that cost three francs a bottle; and the crowning touch, the idea, the true idea, that proved that Monsieur Ibrahim was an expert in the art of screwing the world—replacing the country terrine with dog food.

Thanks to Monsieur Ibrahim's intercession, the adult world cracked, it no longer presented the same rock-solid wall I was always running into; a hand was held out to me through the crack.

I had saved two hundred francs again, and once more I could go and prove to myself that I was a man.

In the Rue de Paradis I went straight to the overhang where my bear's new owner stood. I brought her a shell someone had given me, a real shell that came from the sea, the real sea.

The girl smiled at me.

At that moment a man came running out of the alley fast as a jackrabbit, a whore chasing after him yelling:

"Thief! Thief! My purse!"

Without a moment's hesitation, I stuck out my leg. The thief stumbled a few yards and went sprawling. I jumped on him.

The thief looked at me, saw I was only a kid, smiled, ready to beat me up, but since the girl was charging down the street screaming louder all the time, he got up and cleared out. Fortunately, the prostitute's shouting had given me muscles.

She came closer, teetering on her high heels. I handed her the purse that she clutched delightedly to her luscious bosom so rich in bedroom sounds.

"Thank you, sweetie. What can I do for you? You want me to give you a freebie?"

She was old. Thirty, at least. But Monsieur Ibrahim had always told me not to aggravate a woman.

"OK."

And we went upstairs. My bear's owner looked very offended that her colleague had stolen me from her. When we walked by in front of her, she whispered in my ear:

"Come tomorrow. I'll give you a freebie, too."

I didn't wait for the next day . . .

Monsieur Ibrahim and the whores made life with my father even more difficult. I began to do something terrible, something that baffled me—I was making comparisons. I was always cold when I was around my father. With Monsieur Ibrahim and the prostitutes I felt warmer, lighter.

I would look at the great, lofty library he'd inherited, all those books that supposedly held the quintessence of the human mind, the A to Z of laws, the subtlety of philosophy, and I would look at them in darkness—"Moses, close the shutters, the light will wreck the bindings"—

and then I'd look at my father reading, alone in the circle of the floor lamp that stood over his pages like a yellow conscience. He was enclosed inside the walls of his scholarship, he paid me no more attention than he would a dog—besides, he hated dogs—he wasn't even tempted to throw me one bone of his knowledge. If I made a bit of noise:

"Oh, excuse me."

"Moses, be quiet. I'm reading. I work, you see."

Working, that was the important word, the absolute justification.

"I'm sorry, Dad."

"Ah, it's a good thing your brother Popol wasn't like that."

Popol was the other name for my worthlessness. My father was always throwing the memory of my older brother, Popol, in my face whenever I did something wrong. "Popol really applied himself at school. Popol loved math and he never made the bathtub dirty. Popol didn't pee next to the toilet. Popol liked reading books just as much as Dad."

In the final analysis, it wasn't so bad that my mother had left with Popol not too long after I was born, because fighting a memory was hard enough already, but having to exist side by side with living perfection such as Popol, that would have been too much for me.

"Dad, do you think Popol would have liked me?"

My father stared at me, or rather, in great alarm tried to decode me.

"What a question!"

That's the answer I got: What a question!

I had learned to look at people with my father's eyes. With mistrust and disdain. Talking with the Arab grocer, even if he wasn't an Arab—since in the grocery business, "Arab" means being open nights and Sundays—and doing favors for whores were things I put in a secret drawer of my mind, they weren't officially part of my life.

"Why don't you ever smile, Momo?" Monsieur Ibrahim asked me.

That was a real blow, that question, a punch in the gut, and I wasn't prepared.

"Smiling is something rich folks do, Monsieur Ibrahim. I can't afford it."

Just to piss me off he started to smile.

"You think I'm rich, then?"

"You've got bank notes in your register all the time. I don't know anyone who has so much paper money to look at all day long."

"But these bills are for paying for the merchandise and then the rent as well. And by the end of the month I have very little left over, you know."

And he smiled even more as if to mock me.

"Monsieur Ibrahim, when I tell you that smiling is something rich folks do, I mean that it's for happy people."

"Well now, that's where you're all wrong. It's smiling that makes you happy."

"Yeah, sure."

"Try it."

"Sure, I said."

"You're a polite kid, though, aren't you, Momo?"

"I have to be, or else I get smacked."

"Polite is good. Friendly is better. Try smiling, you'll see."

Fine. After all, when asked nicely by Monsieur Ibrahim, who handed me a can of *choucroute garnie* on the sly, it was worth trying.

The next day, I really behave like a sick person who caught something during the night—I'm smiling at everybody.

"No, Ma'am, I apologize. I didn't understand the math exercise."

Wham—a smile!

"I just couldn't do it."

"Well then, Moses, I'll explain it to you again."

That's a new one. No yelling, no warning. Nothing.

In the lunchroom . . .

"May I have a little more of the chestnut puree, please?"

Wham—a smile!

"Yes, with some cream cheese."

And they give it to me.

In the gym I realize I forgot my gym shoes.

Wham—a smile!

"They weren't dry yet, sir."

The teacher laughs and pats me on the shoulder.

It's intoxicating. Nothing resists me any more. Monsieur Ibrahim has given me the perfect weapon. I'm strafing the whole world with my smile. Nobody is treating me like a pain in the neck any longer.

On the way home from school, I rush to the Rue de Paradis. I approach the most beautiful of the whores, a tall black woman who has always refused me:

"Hey!"

Wham—a smile!

"Shall we go up?"

"Are you sixteen?"

"Of course I'm sixteen. Have been forever!"

Wham—a smile!

We go upstairs.

And afterward, while I get dressed, I tell her that I'm a journalist and that I'm doing a major book about prostitutes.

Wham—a smile!

And that I need her to tell me a little about her life if she wouldn't mind.

"Is that really true? You're a journalist?"

Wham—a smile!

"Yes, well, a journalism student."

She talks to me. I watch her breasts heave gently as she gets enthusiastic. I dare not believe it. A woman is talking to me, to *me*. A woman. Smile. She talks. Smile. She keeps talking.

In the evening when my father comes home, I help him take off his coat as usual, then slip around to face him, standing in the light so that I can be sure he sees me.

"Dinner is ready."

Wham—a smile!

He looks at me in astonishment.

I continue smiling. It's tiring by the end of the day, but I hang in there.

"What did you do? Something stupid, no doubt."

Then the smile disappears.

But I won't despair.

Over dessert I try again.

Wham—a smile!

He stares at me uncomfortably.

"Come here," he says.

I sense that my smile is about to win him over. There we go, another victim. I go over to him. Perhaps he wants to kiss me? One time he told me that Popol really liked to kiss him, that he was a very affectionate boy. Perhaps Popol had understood the smiling trick from birth on? Or maybe my mother had the time to teach him.

I'm close to my father now, leaning against his shoulder. His eyelashes are blinking hard. Me, I'm smiling until it hurts.

"We'll have to get you some braces. I never noticed that your teeth protrude."

That evening I started making it a habit to go and see Monsieur Ibrahim once my father was in bed.

"It's my own fault. If I were more like Popol, my father would love me better."

"How do you know? Popol left."

"So?"

"Perhaps he couldn't stand your father."

"You think so?"

"He left. That proves it, no?"

Monsieur Ibrahim gave me his small change so I could put it into rolls. That calmed me down a little.

"Did you know him? Popol? Monsieur Ibrahim, did you know Popol? What did you think of him, of Popol?"

He hit the cash register once as if to keep it from talking.

"Momo, I'll tell you one thing. I like you a hundred, a thousand times better than Popol."

"Really?"

I was quite thrilled but didn't want to show it. I tightened my fists and bared my teeth a little. Must defend your family.

"Careful! I cannot let you say bad things about my brother. What did you have against Popol?"

"He was all right, Popol, quite all right. But you'll forgive me if I prefer Momo."

I was a good sport: I forgave him.

A week later, Monsieur Ibrahim sent me to see a friend of his, the dentist of the Rue Papillon. He had a lot of influence, Monsieur Ibrahim did, no question about that. And the next day he said to me:

"Momo, smile a little less, it's enough already. No, that was just a joke. . . . My friend assured me that you won't need any braces."

He leaned over to me with his laughing eyes.

"Just imagine, in the Rue de Paradis, you with scrap metal all over your mouth. There wouldn't be a single one of them who'd still believe that you are sixteen."

Now he really hit a bull's-eye, Monsieur Ibrahim. As a result, I asked him for his change so I could calm down.

"How do you know all that, Monsieur Ibrahim?"

"Me, I know nothing. I only know what it says in my Koran."

I made a few more rolls.

"Momo, there's nothing wrong with going to the professionals. The first few times you should always go to professionals, women who know their job really well. Later on, when you get involved and it gets to be more complicated, when feelings are added, then you can make do with amateurs."

I felt better.

"Do you go there sometimes, the Rue de Paradis?"

"Paradise is open to everyone."

"Oh, you're teasing, Monsieur Ibrahim, you're not going to tell me you still go there at your age?"

"Why? Is it reserved for minors only?"

Then I knew I'd said something stupid.

"Momo, how about taking a walk with me?"

"Oh really, you walk sometimes, too?"

And again I knew I'd said something dumb. So I added a huge smile.

"What I mean is that I always see you just sitting on this stool."

I was really excited, though.

The following day, Monsieur Ibrahim took me to Paris, the Paris that is pretty, the one in the photographs, of the tourists. We walked all along the Seine, which isn't really very straight.

"Look, Momo, the Seine loves bridges, like a woman who's crazy about bracelets."

Then we walked through the parks along the Champs-Elysées, between the theaters and the puppet show. Then the Rue du Faubourg–Saint-Honoré, where there were lots of stores with brand names like Lanvin, Hermès, Saint Laurent, and Cardin. It felt odd, these huge and empty shops next to Monsieur Ibrahim's grocery store that was no bigger than a bathroom, but where there wasn't a millimeter that went unused, where every item—vital and not so vital—was piled up from floor to ceiling, from shelf to shelf, three rows high and four rows deep.

"It's crazy, Monsieur Ibrahim, how the shop windows of the rich are so poor. There's nothing in them."

"That's what luxury is, Momo, nothing in the window, nothing in the shop, everything in the price."

We ended with the secret gardens of the Palais-Royal where Monsieur Ibrahim bought me fresh lemonade and rediscovered his legendary immobility on a bar stool, slowly sipping his anise Suze.

"It must be neat to live in Paris."

"But you are living in Paris, Momo."

"No, I live in the Rue Bleue."

I watched him enjoy his anise Suze.

"I thought that Muslims didn't drink alcohol."

"True, but I'm a Sufi."

That's when I sensed I was being indiscreet, that Monsieur Ibrahim didn't want to tell me about his disease—after all, that was his right; I stayed quiet until we were back in the Rue Bleue.

That evening I opened my father's Larousse. I must have been truly worried about Monsieur Ibrahim because, really, dictionaries have always disappointed me.

"*Sufism: a mystical branch of Islam, dating from the eighth century. Opposed to legalism, it emphasizes religion inside the person.*"

There I was, once again! Dictionaries clearly explain only those words you already know.

In any event, Sufism was not a disease, which reassured me somewhat. It was a way of thinking—even if there are ways of thinking that are also diseases, as Monsieur Ibrahim often said. After this I went off on a treasure hunt to try and understand all the words in the definition. From this it became clear that Monsieur Ibrahim with his anise Suze believed in God in the Muslim way, but in a manner that bordered on smuggling for it was "opposed to legalism" and that really gave me a hard time because if legalism was, indeed, the "strict conformity to the law" as the dictionary people were saying . . . well, in general terms that meant disturbing things a priori, namely that Monsieur Ibrahim was dishonest, and thus that the people I frequented were not respectable. But at the same time, if respecting the law was being a lawyer, as my father was, having that gray complexion and so much sadness in the house, I'd rather be against legalism and with Monsieur Ibrahim. And the dictionary people added that Sufism had been created by two ancient guys, al-Halladj and al-Ghazali, names that should be living in the attic rooms in the back of the courtyard—in the Rue Bleue, in any case—and they specified that it was an inner religion and there Monsieur Ibrahim surely was discreet; in comparison to the Jews in the street he was discreet.

During dinner, I couldn't help myself and questioned my father who was busy gulping down a lamb stew, Royal Canine style.

"Dad, do you believe in God?"

He looked at me. Then, slowly, he said:

"I can see that you're becoming a man."

I didn't get the connection. For a moment I even wondered if someone had reported to him that I was seeing the girls of the Rue de Paradis. But then he added:

"No, I've never managed to believe in God."

"Never managed? Why? Does one have to make an effort?"

He looked around at the semi-darkness of the apartment.

"To believe that all this has any meaning? Yes. You have to make an enormous effort."

"But Dad, we're Jews. Well, you and I, aren't we?"

"Yes."

"And being Jewish has nothing to do with God?"

"For me it no longer does. Being Jewish is merely having memories. Bad memories."

And then his face really looked like that of someone in desperate need of aspirin. Maybe because he had been talking for a change, which was unusual for him, not one of his habits. He got up and went straight to bed.

A few days later, he came home looking even paler than usual. I was beginning to feel guilty. I told myself that by making him eat shitty stuff I had perhaps derailed his health.

I sat down and he motioned to me that he wanted to tell me something.

But it took him a good ten minutes to get around to it.

"I've been fired, Moses. They don't want me any more in the office where I work."

Frankly, it didn't really surprise me that they didn't feel like working with my father—for the criminals he must have been depressing to be with—but at the same time I had never imagined that a lawyer could stop being a lawyer.

"I'll have to look for other work. Somewhere else. We'll have to tighten the belt, my son."

He went off to bed. Obviously, he wasn't interested in knowing what I was thinking.

I went down to see Monsieur Ibrahim, who was smiling and chewing peanuts.

"How do you manage to be so happy, Monsieur Ibrahim?"

"I know what it says in my Koran."

"Maybe I should swipe that from you one day, your Koran, that is. Even if that's not done when you're Jewish."

"Phew, what does it mean to you, Momo, being Jewish?"

"Well, I don't know. For my father it means being depressed all day. For me . . . it's just something that keeps me from being anything else."

Monsieur Ibrahim gave me a peanut.

"Your shoes are in bad shape, Momo. Tomorrow we'll go and buy you some new shoes."

"Yes, but . . ."

"A man spends his life in just two places—either in his bed or in his shoes."

"I have no money, Monsieur Ibrahim."

"They're a present. It's my gift to you, Momo. You have only one pair of feet and you should take care of them. If shoes hurt you, you must change them. Feet can't be changed!"

The next day, coming home from school, I found a note on the floor of our unlit entryway. I don't know why but at the sight of my father's handwriting, my heart beat madly in all directions:

Moses,
Forgive me, but I am leaving. I don't have it in me to be a father. Popo . . .

The next part was crossed out. Without any doubt he had wanted to pitch me a sentence about Popol. In the style of "with Popol I would have managed, but not with you," or maybe "Popol gave me the strength and energy to be a father, but not you"—in short, some crappy thing he was ashamed to write down. Well, I sure got the message, thank you.

Perhaps we will see each other again one day, later on, when you're grown. When I am less ashamed and you have forgiven me.

That's it, farewell!

P.S. I left all the money I have on the table. Here's a list of people whom you should inform of my departure. They will take care of you.

Then there followed a list of four names I did not recognize.

My decision was made. I would have to pretend.

Admitting that I had been abandoned was out of the question. Twice abandoned—once by my mother when I was born, and again as an adolescent by my father. If this became known, there wouldn't be anyone left who would give me a chance. What was so terrible about me? What was so wrong with me that made love impossible? My decision was irrevocable—I would disguise my father's absence. I would make people believe he was there, he ate there, and that he still shared his long and boring evenings with me.

In fact, I didn't wait at all—I went down to the grocery store.

"Monsieur Ibrahim, my father has indigestion. What should I give him?"

"Fernet Branca, Momo. Here, I have a little bottle right here."

"Thank you. I'll run back up and have him take it right away."

With the money he had left me, I could manage for a month. I learned to imitate his signature to complete the necessary mail and respond to the lycée. I continued cooking for two and every night I set his place at the table across from me; the only difference was that at the end of the meal I would throw his down the sink.

A few nights a week, just for the neighbors across the street, I'd sit in his armchair, wear his sweater and shoes, put some flour in my hair, and try to read a brand-new Koran Monsieur Ibrahim had given me because I had begged him for one.

At school I told myself I didn't have a moment to lose—I had to fall in love. There wasn't much choice there since the school was not coed. All the boys were in love with Myriam, the concierge's daughter, who despite her thirteen years had very rapidly understood that she was reigning over three hundred starved adolescents. I started courting her with the fervor of a drowning man.

Wham—a smile!

I had to prove to myself that I could be loved. I had to let the whole world know before they discovered that even my parents, the only ones who were obliged to put up with me, had preferred escape.

I told Monsieur Ibrahim of my conquest of Myriam. He listened to me with the little smile of someone who knows how the story ends, but I pretended not to notice.

"And how's your father? I don't see him in the mornings any more."

"He's got a lot of work. He has to leave very early now with his new job."

"Oh really? And he isn't furious about your reading the Koran?"

"I do it secretly, anyway. And besides, I don't understand very much of what's in it."

"When you want to learn something, you don't take a book. You talk to someone. I don't believe in books."

"But still, Monsieur Ibrahim, you're always telling me that you know what . . ."

"Yes, that I know what it says in my Koran. Momo, I feel like seeing the sea. What if we went to Normandy? I'll take you."

"Would you really?"

"If your father agrees, of course."

"He'll agree."

"Are you sure?"

"I'm telling you, he'll agree."

When we arrived in the lobby of the Grand Hotel in Cabourg, it was all too much for me—I began to cry. I cried for two or maybe three hours, I could barely stop to catch my breath.

Monsieur Ibrahim watched me cry. He waited patiently for me to start speaking. Finally I managed to blurt out:

"It's too beautiful here, Monsieur Ibrahim. It's much too beautiful. It's not for me. I don't deserve this."

Monsieur Ibrahim smiled.

"Beauty is everywhere, Momo. Wherever you turn your eyes. Now, that comes from my Koran."

Then we went for a walk along the shore.

"You know, Momo, if a man hasn't had life revealed to him directly by God, he's not going to find it in a book."

I talked to him about Myriam, all the more so because I was trying to avoid talking about my father. Having admitted me into her circle of suitors, Myriam was now beginning to reject me as an unworthy candidate.

"It doesn't matter," Monsieur Ibrahim said. "Your love for her belongs to you. It's yours. Even if she refuses it, she cannot change it. She isn't benefiting from it, that's all. What you give, Momo, is yours forever. What you keep is lost for all time!"

"But you, do you have a wife?"

"Yes."

"And why then aren't you here with her?"

He pointed to the sea.

"This really is an English sea right here, green and gray. These are not the normal colors of water. You'd think they'd taken on an accent."

"You didn't answer me, Monsieur Ibrahim, about your wife. About your wife?"

"Momo, no answer is also an answer."

Each morning, Monsieur Ibrahim was up first. He'd go to the window, sniff the light, and slowly do his exercises—every morning, his whole life through, morning exercises. He was incredibly flexible and as I opened my eyes I could still see, from my pillow, the tall and carefree young man he must have been, very long ago.

A great surprise to me was discovering in the bathroom one day that Monsieur Ibrahim was circumcised.

"You, too, Monsieur Ibrahim?"

"Muslims just like Jews, Momo. It's about the sacrifice of Abraham: he holds his child out to God, telling him he may take him. That bit of skin that we don't have is the mark of Abraham. At the circumcision, the father must hold his son, the father offers his own pain in memory of Abraham's sacrifice."

Through Monsieur Ibrahim, I realized that Jews, Muslims, and even Christians had plenty of great men in common before they began to beat up on each other. It didn't concern me, but it did me good.

After our return from Normandy, when I came home to the dark and empty apartment, I didn't feel different but I did sense that the world could be different. I told myself that I could open the windows, that the walls could be lighter. I said to myself that nothing forced me to keep this furniture that smelled of the past, not the good old days, no, the worn and rancid days, those that smell like an old floor cloth.

I had no money left. I began to sell the books in lots to the book vendors on the banks of the Seine that Monsieur Ibrahim had shown me during our walks. Every time I sold a book I felt freer.

It was three months now since my father had vanished. I was still pretending, keeping up appearances, still cooking for two, and strangely enough Monsieur Ibrahim asked after my father less and less frequently. My relationship with Myriam crumbled more and more, but it provided me with a very good topic of conversation for the evenings with Monsieur Ibrahim.

Some nights I felt my heart shrink. That was because I was thinking of Popol. Now that my father was no longer there, I would have liked to get to know Popol. I was sure that I would be better able to stand him since he was no longer being thrown in my face as the antithesis to my worthlessness. I often went to bed thinking that somewhere in the world there was a good-looking and perfect brother who was unknown to me and that maybe I would meet him one day.

One morning the police knocked on the door. They were shouting as they do in movies:

"Open up! Police!"

I said to myself, "OK, that's it, it's all over. I've been lying too much. They're coming to arrest me."

I put on a robe and unlocked all the bolts. They looked a lot less mean than I'd imagined, they even asked me politely if they could come in. True, I myself, too, preferred getting dressed before leaving for prison.

In the living room, the inspector took my hand and said very gently:

"Young man, we have some bad news for you. Your father is dead."

I didn't know right away what astonished me more, my father's death or the formal way the cop was addressing me. In any case, I collapsed into the armchair.

"He threw himself under a train near Marseille."

That was very strange, as well—why go all the way to Marseille! There are trains everywhere. There are just as many, if not more, in Paris itself. I really would never understand my father.

"There is every indication that your father was desperate and ended his life of his own free will."

A father who commits suicide, now that was something that wasn't going to make me feel any better. Finally, I wondered if I wouldn't rather have a father who deserts me; at least I could assume that he was being eaten up by remorse.

The officers seemed to understand my silence. They were looking at the empty library, the somber apartment, and must have been thinking how, thankfully, they'd be out of here in just a few more minutes.

"Who should we notify, my boy?"

That's when I had an appropriate reaction at last. I got up and went to look for the list with the four names he had left me. The inspector put it in his pocket.

"We'll give this information to Social Services."

Then he came over to me with his hangdog eyes and I could tell he had something hideous for me.

"Now, I have to ask something delicate: you will have to identify the body."

That played like an alarm signal. I began to shriek as if someone had pressed the button. The officers were churning around me looking to turn it off. Only, no luck, because the off-button was me and I couldn't stop myself any more.

Monsieur Ibrahim was fantastic. When he heard my screams he came upstairs and instantly grasped the situation. He said that he would go to Marseille himself and identify the body. At first, the police were suspicious because he really did look like an Arab, but I began to shriek again and then they accepted Monsieur Ibrahim's suggestion.

After the burial, I asked Monsieur Ibrahim:

"How long have you known about my father, Monsieur Ibrahim?"

"Since Cabourg. But you know, Momo, you shouldn't hold it against your father."

"Really? How so? A father who ruins my life, abandons me, and then commits suicide. That's a hell of a lot of trust to give someone to live by. And then, to boot, I'm not supposed to hold it against him?"

"Your father had no model to follow. He lost his parents when he was very young because they'd been taken away by the Nazis and died in the camps. Your father never got over having escaped all that. Maybe he felt guilty about being alive. It's not for nothing that he ended up under a train."

"Oh really, why?"

"His parents had been taken away by a train to go to their death. Perhaps he had been looking for his train all along. . . . If he didn't have the strength to live it was not because of you, Momo, but because of everything that did or did not happen before you."

Then Monsieur Ibrahim stuffed some bills into my pocket.

"Here, go to the Rue de Paradis. The girls have been wondering where you're at with that book about them."

I began to change everything in the apartment in the Rue Bleue. Monsieur Ibrahim gave me cans of paint and brushes. He also gave me advice on how to make the social worker crazy and play for time.

One afternoon when I'd opened all the windows wide to let the smell of the acrylic paint out, a woman entered the apartment. I don't know why, but I knew right away who she was from her embarrassment, her hesitation, and the way she didn't dare walk between the ladders and was avoiding the spots on the floor.

I pretended to be deeply immersed in the work.

She finally cleared her throat softly.

I acted surprised:

"You're looking for?"

"I'm looking for Moses," said my mother.

It was odd how she had a hard time pronouncing the name as if she couldn't get it out of her mouth.

I took the luxury of screwing around with her.

"And who are you?"

"I'm his mother."

Poor woman, I felt pity for her. The state she was in. She must have really forced herself to get to this point.

She looks at me intently, trying to scan my features. She is scared, very scared.

"And who are you?"

"Me?"

I feel like having fun. It's incredible how people can get themselves in such a state, especially after thirteen years.

"Me, they call me Momo."

Her face shatters.

Laughing, I add:

"It's a diminutive for Mohammed."

She becomes even paler than the paint on my baseboards.

"Oh really? You're not Moses?"

"Oh no, you shouldn't confuse the two, Madame. Me, I'm Mohammed."

She swallows her saliva. She's not really unhappy about it when all is said and done.

"But isn't there a boy here whose name is Moses?"

I feel like answering: "I don't know, you're his mother, you ought to know." But at the last moment I hold it in because the poor woman doesn't look very steady on her legs. Instead, I make up a pretty and more comfortable little lie.

"Moses left, Madame. He'd had enough of all of this. He didn't have any good memories."

"Oh really?"

I'm wondering if she believes me. She doesn't seem convinced. Maybe she isn't so stupid after all.

"And when will he be back?"

"I don't know. When he left he said he wanted to find his brother."

"His brother?"

"Yes, Moses has a brother."

"Oh really?"

She looks utterly bewildered.

"Yes, his brother Popol."

"Popol?"

"Yes, Madame. Popol, his older brother."

I'm wondering if perhaps she is taking me for a simpleton. Or else she really believes I'm Mohammed.

"But I never had a child before Moses. I never had any Popol."

Now I'm beginning to feel bad.

She notices it, she is shaking so much that she has to sit down in an armchair and I do the same.

We look at each other in silence, our noses stuffed with the sharp smell of acrylic. She studies me, and there's not a blink of my eyes that escapes her.

"Tell me, Momo . . ."

"Mohammed."

"Tell me, Mohammed, will you be seeing Moses again?"

"Possibly."

I say it in a detached tone, I can't get over the detachment in my voice. She scrutinizes me, looks deep into my eyes. She can pick at me as much as she wants, she won't get anything out of me, I'm very sure of myself.

"If you should see Moses again one day, tell him that I was very young when I married his father, and that I married him only to get away from my parents. I never loved Moses' father. But I was ready to love Moses. Only, I met another man. Your father . . ."

"Excuse me?"

"I mean his father, Moses' father, said to me: 'Go, then, but leave Moses with me, or else. . . .' So I left. I preferred to make my life over, a life where there would be some happiness."

"It's better that way, that's for sure."

She lowers her eyes.

She comes over to me. I sense she would like to kiss me. I act as if I don't understand. In an imploring voice she asks me:

"You will tell Moses, won't you?"

"Perhaps."

That same evening, I went back to Monsieur Ibrahim and asked him laughingly:

"So when are you going to adopt me, Monsieur Ibrahim?"

And he answered, laughing also:

"Well, tomorrow if you want, my little Momo."

We had to fight for it. The official world, the one with its stamps, authorizations, and its civil servants who become aggressive when you wake them up. Nobody wanted anything to do with us. But Monsieur Ibrahim was not to be discouraged.

"We already have the no in our pocket, Momo. We have to acquire the yes."

My mother, with the help of the social worker, ended up by going along with Monsieur Ibrahim's efforts.

"And what about your wife, Monsieur Ibrahim?" I asked. "Has she agreed?"

"My wife went back to the old country a long time ago. I do what I want. But if you'd like to, we can go and see her this summer."

The day we obtained it, the document, the famous document that declared I was henceforth the son of the man I had chosen, Monsieur Ibrahim decided that we should buy a car to celebrate.

"We'll take trips, Momo. And this summer, we'll go to the Golden Crescent together. I will show you the sea, the one and only sea, the sea where I come from."

"Couldn't we go there by flying carpet maybe?"

"Take some brochures and choose a car."

"Yes, Dad."

It's weird how you can have very different feelings using the same words. When I said "Dad" to Monsieur Ibrahim, my heart was smiling, I swelled with pride, and the future was shimmering.

We went to the garage owner.

"I want to buy this model. It's the one my son chose."

As for Monsieur Ibrahim, he was worse than I when it came to the question of vocabulary. He was adding "my son" to every sentence, as if he had just invented fatherhood.

The salesman started to carry on about the features of the motor.

"Don't bother trying to sell me the item. I already told you I want to buy it."

"Do you have a license, sir?"

"Of course."

And then Monsieur Ibrahim took a document out of his Moroccan leather wallet that must have, at the very least, dated from the Egyptian era. The salesman examined the papyrus with horror, first of all because most of the letters were washed out, and second because it was in a language he didn't know.

"Is this thing a driver's license?"

"Isn't that obvious?"

"Fine. Well then, we suggest that you pay in several monthly installments. For instance, over a period of three years, you should . . ."

"When I tell you that I want to purchase a car, it's because I can afford to do so. I'm paying in cash."

Monsieur Ibrahim was very annoyed. The salesman was really committing one blunder after another.

"Well then, write us a check . . ."

"That's enough! I'm telling you I'm paying cash. With money. Real money."

And he put wads of bank notes on the table, lovely wads of old notes neatly packed in plastic bags.

The salesman almost choked.

"But . . . but . . . nobody pays in cash . . . that . . . that's not possible . . ."

"Well, what's the problem? Are you saying this is not money then? I certainly accepted them in my cash register, so why shouldn't you? Momo, is this a serious outfit we've come to?"

"Fine. We'll do it your way. We shall make the car available to you in two weeks."

"Two weeks? That's impossible—I'll be dead by then!"

Two days later, they delivered the car to the grocery store. He's really something, Monsieur Ibrahim.

When he got into the car, Monsieur Ibrahim began to touch the various controls carefully with his long and slender fingers; then he wiped his forehead, turning green.

"I don't know how anymore, Momo."

"But didn't you learn?"

"Yes, a long time ago, from my friend Abdullah. But . . ."

"But?"

"But cars were different then."

He really was having a hard time knowing what to say or do.

"Tell me, Monsieur Ibrahim, the kind of cars you learned in, were they horse-drawn?"

"No, my little Momo. Donkeys. Drawn by donkeys."

"And that driver's license the other day, what was that?"

"Hmm . . . an old letter from my friend Abdullah, telling me how the harvest had been."

"Well, we're up shit's creek!"

"You said it, Momo."

"And there's nothing in your Koran that would offer a solution, as always?"

"What are you thinking, Momo, that the Koran is a driver's manual? It's useful for things of the spirit, not for scrap iron. And besides, in the Koran they travel by camel!"

"Don't get all worked up, Monsieur Ibrahim."

In the end, Monsieur Ibrahim decided that we should take driving lessons together. Since I wasn't old enough yet, he was the one who officially was learning while I sat in the back seat without missing one iota of the teacher's instructions. As soon as the lesson was over, we'd take our car and I would be in the driver's seat. We'd ride around Paris by night to avoid the traffic.

I was getting better and better at it.

At last summer arrived and we took to the road.

Thousands of miles. We crossed all of Europe by the southern route. Windows open. We were going to the Middle East. It was an unbelievable discovery to see how interesting the universe became as soon as you traveled with Monsieur Ibrahim. Since I was clutching the steering wheel and concentrating on the road, he would describe the landscapes, sky, clouds, villages, and people to me. Monsieur Ibrahim's chatter, his voice as thin as cigarette paper, the flavor of his accent, the images, exclamations, and surprises, followed by the most diabolical tricks, all that is what the road from

Paris to Istanbul means to me. I did not see Europe, I heard it.

"Oh, now, Momo, we've reached the affluent—look, there are garbage cans."

"Garbage cans, so what?"

"When you want to know whether you're in a rich or poor area, you should look at the garbage cans. If you see garbage cans but no trash, it's wealthy. If you see trash next to the garbage cans, then it's neither rich nor poor— it's a tourist district. If you see trash without any garbage cans, then it's poor. And if the people live in the trash, then it's very, very poor, indeed. Here we're in a rich area."

"Well sure, it's Switzerland."

"Oh no, Momo, not the highway. All the highway is good for is to tell you to keep moving, there's nothing to see. That's for idiots who want to go as fast as possible from one point to another. We're not doing geometry here, we're traveling. Find me some pretty little roads that show us all there is to see."

"You can tell it's not you who is doing the driving, Monsieur Ibrahim."

"Listen, Momo, if you don't want to see anything, then you take a plane, like everyone else."

"Is it poor here, Monsieur Ibrahim?"

"Yes, this is Albania."

"And there?"

"Stop the car. You smell this? It smells of happiness, this is Greece. People don't move, they take the time to watch us pass by, they breathe. You see, Momo, all my life I worked hard, but I worked slowly, taking my time. I didn't just want to ring up numbers or watch the customers parade in and out, no. Slowness, that's the secret of happiness. What do you want to do later on?"

"Don't know, Monsieur Ibrahim. Yes, I do. I'll work in import-export."

Now I'd scored a point. I had found the magic word. Monsieur Ibrahim couldn't stop talking about import-export. It was a serious word and yet adventurous, a word that evoked journeys, ships, packages, big turnovers, a word as heavy as the syllables that it rolled over—*import-export!*

"Let me introduce my son Momo to you, who will be in import-export one day."

We had plenty of games. He had me go into religious places blindfolded so that I would guess the religion by its scent.

"It smells like candles here. It's Catholic."

"Yes, it is Saint Anthony."

"This is incense. It's orthodox."

"You're right, it's Saint Sophia."

"And here it smells like feet. It's Muslim. But I mean, really, it stinks too much . . ."

"What! It's the Blue Mosque! A place that smells of human bodies isn't good enough for you? Is that because your feet never smell? A place of prayer that smells of men, is made for men, with men inside, that's disgusting to you? You really have some very Parisian ideas, don't you! I find the smell of socks comforting. I remind myself that I am no better than my neighbor. I smell myself, I smell us, and so I already feel better!"

From Istanbul on, Monsieur Ibrahim talked less. He was deeply moved.

"Soon we will reach the sea where I am from."

Each day he wanted us to drive more slowly. He wanted to savor it all. He was afraid, also.

"Where is that sea that you come from, Monsieur Ibrahim? Show me on the map."

"Oh, don't bother me with your maps, Momo. We're not in high school now!"

We stopped in a mountain village.

"I'm happy, Momo. You're here and I know what it says in my Koran. Now I want to take you out dancing."

"Dancing, Monsieur Ibrahim?"

"We have to. Absolutely. 'A man's heart is like a bird locked inside the cage of the body.' When you dance, the heart sings like a bird aspiring to a fusion with God. Come, let's go to the *tekké*."

"To the what?"

"Strange club!" I said as we came through the door.

"A *tekké* is not a club. It's a monastery. Momo, take off your shoes and put them down."

And that is where I saw men whirl for the first time. The dervishes wore large pale robes, heavy and soft. A drum reverberated. And then the monks turned into spinning tops.

"You see, Momo! They're whirling around, they're turning around their own heart, the place where God is present. It's like a prayer."

"You call that a prayer?"

"Of course, Momo. They lose every earthly reference point, the heaviness we call equilibrium, and they become torches that are consumed in a huge fire. Try it, Momo, just try it. Follow me."

And Monsieur Ibrahim and I began to whirl.

With the first few rounds, I said to myself:

I am happy with Monsieur Ibrahim. Then I thought: *I'm no longer angry with my father for having left.* In the end, I even thought: *After all, my mother didn't really have any choice when she . . .*

"So, Momo, did you feel good things?"

"Yeah, it was incredible. My hate was draining away. If the drums hadn't stopped I might have tried to justify my mother's case. It was really nice to pray, Monsieur Ibrahim, even though I would have liked praying better with my sneakers on. The heavier the body becomes, the lighter the spirit."

After that day, we stopped often to dance in *tekkés* Monsieur Ibrahim was familiar with. Sometimes he didn't whirl and was just happy to have some tea with his eyes half-closed, but I would whirl like a madman. No, actually I was whirling to become a little less mad.

In the evening in the village squares, I tried to talk to the girls a bit. I did my utmost but it wasn't going terribly well, while Monsieur Ibrahim did nothing but drink his anise Suze and smile with that sweet and calm look of his and, well, within an hour he always had lots of people around him.

"You move too much, Momo. If you want to have friends, you shouldn't budge."

"Monsieur Ibrahim, do you think I'm good-looking?"

"You're very handsome, Momo."

"No, that's not what I mean. Do you think that I'll be good-looking enough to attract any girls . . . without having to pay?"

"In a few years they will be paying for you!"

"Still . . . for now . . . it's all rather quiet."

"Obviously, Momo, have you noticed how you're going about it? You stare at them as if wanting to say: 'See how handsome I am.' Well, of course they laugh. You should look at them as if you want to say: 'I've never seen anyone more beautiful than you.' For an ordinary man, I mean a man like you and me—not Alain Delon or Marlon Brando—your looks are what you find in the woman."

We watched the sun slide between the mountains and the sky turn violet. Dad stared at the evening star.

"A ladder has been placed before us by which to escape, Momo. First man was mineral, then vegetable, then animal—and he can't forget the animal part, and often has a tendency to be one again—then he became man, endowed with knowledge, reason, and faith. Can you imagine the distance you've already covered, from dust to today? And later, when you have gone beyond your human condition, you will become an angel. You'll be done with earth. When you dance, you have a foretaste of that."

"Maybe. I, for one, don't remember anything. Do you remember having been a plant, Monsieur Ibrahim?"

"Well, what do you think I'm doing when I sit there without moving for hours on my stool in the grocery store?"

Then the famous day arrived that Monsieur Ibrahim announced we were going to the sea of his birth to meet his friend Abdullah. He was completely nonplussed, like a young man. He wanted to go there by himself first to find the place, and asked me to wait for him under an olive tree.

It was siesta time. I fell asleep against the tree.

When I woke up, the day was gone. I waited for Monsieur Ibrahim until midnight.

I walked to the next village. When I reached the square, people rushed over to me. I didn't understand their language, but they were speaking very excitedly and seemed to know me very well. They brought me to a large house. First I went through a long room where several women were crouching and moaning. Then they brought me to Monsieur Ibrahim.

He was lying down, covered with wounds, bruises, and blood. The car had run into a wall.

He looked terribly weak.

I threw myself upon him. He opened his eyes and smiled.

"Momo, this is where the journey ends."

"Oh no, we haven't arrived there yet, at the sea of your birth."

"Yes, I'm there. Every branch of the river comes out into the same sea. The one and only sea."

Then, in spite of myself, I began to weep.

"Momo, I'm not happy."

"I'm afraid for you, Monsieur Ibrahim."

"Me, I'm not afraid, Momo. I know what it says in my Koran."

That was a sentence he shouldn't have spoken. It brought back too many good memories, and so I began to sob even more.

"Momo, you are crying for yourself, not for me. I have lived a good life. I have lived to be old. I have had a wife who died a very long time ago but whom I still love just as much. I had my friend Abdullah, and you will give him my warmest greetings. My little grocery store did well. The Rue Bleue is a nice street even if it isn't blue. And then there was you."

Just to please him, I swallowed the rest of my tears and made an effort and wham—a smile!

He was happy. It seemed he was in less pain.

Wham—a smile!

He gently closed his eyes.

"Monsieur Ibrahim!"

"Shh . . . don't worry. I'm not dying, Momo, I'm going to join infinity."

There it is.

I stayed for a while. I spoke about Dad a lot with his friend Abdullah. We did a lot of whirling, too.

Monsieur Abdullah was like Monsieur Ibrahim, but a parchment version of Monsieur Ibrahim, full of unusual words and poems that he knew by heart, a Monsieur Ibrahim who had spent more time reading than making his cash register ring. He called the hours that we spent whirling in the *tekké* the dance of alchemy, the dance that changes copper into gold. He often quoted Rumi and would say:

Gold does not need the philosopher's stone but copper does.

Improve yourself.

Let die what is alive: that is your body.

Revive what is dead: that is your heart.

Hide what is present: that is the world down here.

Let come what is absent: that is the world of the future life.

Annihilate what exists: that is passion.

Produce what does not exist: that is intention.

Thus, even today, when things are going badly, I whirl.

I turn one hand toward the sky and I whirl. I turn one hand toward the floor and I whirl. The sky turns above me. The earth turns below me. I am no longer myself but one of those atoms that turns around the void that is everything.

As Monsieur Ibrahim used to say:

"Your intelligence is in your ankles and your ankles have a very profound way of thinking."

I hitchhiked back. I put myself into "the hands of God," as Monsieur Ibrahim used to say when he was talking about the homeless. I begged and I slept under the open sky and that, too, was quite a beautiful gift. I didn't want to spend the money Monsieur Abdullah had slipped into my pocket when he kissed me just before I left him.

Back in Paris, I discovered that Monsieur Ibrahim had anticipated everything. He had emancipated me and so I was free. I inherited his money, his grocery store, and his Koran.

The lawyer handed me the gray envelope and I tenderly took out the old book. At last I was going to find out what it said in his Koran.

In his Koran were two dried flowers and a letter from his friend Abdullah.

Now I am Momo and everybody in the street knows me. In the end I didn't go into import-export, which I had said only to make a bit of an impression on Monsieur Ibrahim.

From time to time my mother comes to see me. She calls me Mohammed so that I won't get angry and she asks me for news from Moses, which I give her.

Recently, I told her that Moses had found his brother Popol again and they had left on a trip together and that, as far as I could tell, we wouldn't see them any time soon. Perhaps it wasn't worth discussing any more. She thought for a long time—she is always on her guard with me—then she murmured gently:

"After all, maybe it's better that way. There are some forms of childhood you should leave behind, that need healing."

I told her psychology wasn't my field; the grocery store was who I was.

"I'd like to invite you for dinner one evening, Mohammed. My husband would like to meet you, too."

"What does he do?"

"He teaches English."

"And you?"

"I teach Spanish."

"And what language do we speak at dinner? No, I was just joking, I'd like that."

She flushed pink with delight that I had accepted. No, really it's true, it was a pleasure to watch—you would have thought I had just installed running water for her.

"Really, you mean it? You'll come?"

"Yeah, yeah."

What is certain is that it is a little strange to have two teachers from the state education system receive Mohammed, the grocer, but then again, why not? I'm not racist.

There it is . . . it's become a habit. I go to their house every Monday with my wife and children. They're so affectionate, my kids, they call her—the Spanish teacher—Grandmama and you should see how that thrills her! Sometimes she is so elated that she gingerly asks me if it doesn't bother me. I tell her no, that I have a sense of humor.

So, now I am Momo, the one who has the grocery store in the Rue Bleue, the Rue Bleue that isn't blue.

In everybody's eyes I am the local Arab.

In the grocery business, being Arab means being open at night and on Sundays.

Oscar and
the Lady in Pink

❧

For Danielle Darrieux

Dear God,

My name is Oscar. I am ten years old. I've set the cat on fire, and the dog, and the house (I think I even roasted the goldfish), and this is the first letter I've ever sent you because until now I didn't have any time since I had to study.

I'll tell you right off the bat: I hate writing. I really have to be forced. Because writing is just decoration, trinkets, silly smiles, ribbons, and so on. Writing is nothing but prettified lying. Something grown-ups do.

You want proof? Well, look at the way my letter starts out: "My name is Oscar. I am ten years old. I've set the cat on fire, and the dog, and the house (I think I even roasted the goldfish), and this is the first letter I'm sending you because until now I didn't have any time since I had to study." I could just as well have put: "They call me Bald Egg, I look only seven years old, I live at the hospital because of my cancer, and I've never talked to you before because I don't even think you exist."

But if I write that, it'll make a lousy impression and you won't be interested in me. And I need you to be interested.

It would be really nice, actually, if you had time to do me two or three favors.

Let me explain.

The hospital is a super-cool place with lots of grown-ups who're always in a good mood and talk loud. There are lots of toys and ladies in pink, they wear pink you see, who want to have a good time with the children, with buddies like Bacon, Einstein, or Popcorn, who're always available, so the hospital is really great if you're a patient who's nice.

I'm not so nice anymore. Since my bone-marrow transplant I can tell I'm not nice anymore. When Dr. Düsseldorf examines me in the morning, his heart isn't in it any longer. I'm a disappointment to him. He looks at me and says nothing, as if I'd done something wrong. But I really did do my best when I had the operation; I was good, I let them put me to sleep, when it hurt I didn't cry out, and I took all my medicine. Some days I really feel like yelling at him, telling him, this Dr. Düsseldorf and his black eyebrows, that perhaps it's his own fault that the operation failed. But he looks so unhappy that the insults get stuck in my throat. The more silent Dr. Düsseldorf and his sad look are, the guiltier I feel. I know I've become a bad patient, one of those who keep others from thinking medicine is always fantastic.

What a doctor thinks is contagious. Now the whole floor, nurses, interns, housekeepers, they all look at me the same way. They seem sad when I'm in a good mood; they force themselves to laugh when I tell a joke. It's really true, we don't have fun like before.

Only Mamie-Rose hasn't changed. As far as I can tell, she's too old to change anyway. And besides, she's just too much Mamie-Rose as well. I won't introduce Mamie-Rose to you, God, she's a good buddy of yours already, considering she's the one who told me to write to you. The problem is that I'm the only one who calls her Mamie-Rose. So you'll have to try hard to figure out who it is I'm talking about: she is the oldest of all the ladies who wear pink and who come from the outside to spend time with the children who're sick.

"How old are you, Mamie-Rose?"

"Can you remember numbers of thirteen digits, Oscar, my little friend?"

"Oh! You're kidding!"

"No, I'm not. And they really mustn't find out what my age is here or else they'll let me go and we won't see each other any more."

"Why?"

"I've been smuggled in here. There's an age limit for the ladies in pink. And I'm way beyond that."

"Have you gone bad?"

"Yes."

"Like yogurt?"

"Shhh!"

"OK! I won't say a word."

She was really very courageous to admit her secret to me. But she's in good hands with me. I sure will be quiet about it, although I find it surprising that nobody has suspected anything considering all the wrinkles she has around her eyes, like rays of sun.

A different time I found out another one of her secrets and with that one, God, I'm sure you'll be able to identify her.

We were walking around the hospital garden and she stepped in some poop.

"Shit!"

"Mamie-Rose! You're saying a dirty word!"

"Oh, come on kid, leave me alone. I'll say whatever I want."

"Oh Mamie-Rose!"

"And move your butt. We're taking a walk, we're not ambling along like snails."

When we sat down on a bench to have a piece of candy, I asked:

"How come you use such bad words?"

"Professional habit, my little Oscar. In my job I would've been in deep trouble if my vocabulary had been too proper."

"And what job was that?"

"You won't believe me . . ."

"I swear to you that I will."

"Wrestling."

"I don't believe you!"

"I was a wrestler! They nicknamed me the Strangler of Languedoc."

Since that day, whenever I'm feeling a little low and she's sure there's no one around who can hear us, Mamie-Rose tells me all about her big matches—the Strangler of Languedoc against the Lady Butcher of Limousin, her twenty-year-long fight against Diabolica Sinclair, a Dutch woman who had cannon shells instead of breasts, and above all her world cup against Ulla-Ulla, known as the Bitch of Büchenwald who'd never been beaten, not even by Steel Thighs, who was Mamie-Rose's great model when she was a wrestler. They make me dream those fights of hers, because I imagine my friend in the ring as she is today, a little old lady in a pink shirt, a little wobbly, and all the while beating the hell out of giant women in leotards. I'm thinking it's me. I grow stronger. I take my revenge.

Well, God, if with all this information—Mamie-Rose or the Strangler of Languedoc—you don't know who Mamie-Rose is, then you should stop being God and retire. I think I've been clear enough, no?

Let me get back to my own stuff.

In short, my transplant has been a real disappointment here. My chemo, too, was disappointing but less so because they had high hopes for the transplant. Now I have the feeling the doctors don't know what to suggest next. It's pitiful to see. Dr. Düsseldorf, who my mother thinks is so handsome, although I find his eyebrows too big, looks as distressed as a Santa Claus with no presents left in his sack.

The atmosphere is getting worse. I spoke with my friend Bacon about it. His name is actually not Bacon but Yves, but we call him Bacon because it suits him much better since he's so badly burned.

"Bacon, I have the feeling the doctors don't like me any more. I make them depressed."

"No joke, Bald Egg! Doctors, they're for the birds. They're always ready to do surgery on you. Me, I figure they've promised me at least six operations already."

"Maybe you inspire them."

"Yeah, sure."

"But why don't they just tell me I'm going to die?"

At that point Bacon, like everyone else in the hospital, became deaf. If you say the word "die" in a hospital, nobody hears it. You can be sure there'll be an air pocket and they'll start talking about something else. I've tested it on everybody. Except Mamie-Rose.

So this morning I wanted to check and see if she, too, was going to become hard of hearing when I mentioned it.

"Mamie-Rose, I've got the feeling that nobody is telling me I'm going to die."

She looks at me. Will she react just like the others? Please, Strangler of Languedoc, resist and keep your hearing!

"Why do you want them to tell you if you already know, Oscar?"

Phew, she heard.

"I've the feeling, Mamie-Rose, they invented a hospital different from the one that really exists. They act as if you go to a hospital just to get better. But you go there to die, too."

"You're right, Oscar. And I believe they make the same mistake with life. We forget that life is fragile, brittle, ephemeral. We all pretend we're immortal."

"My operation didn't work, did it, Mamie-Rose?"

Mamie-Rose didn't answer. That was her way of agreeing with me. When she was sure I'd understood, she came closer and asked me in an anxious voice:

"Of course, I never told you anything. Swear to me?"

"Promise."

We stayed silent for a moment, a question of thoroughly digesting all these new thoughts.

"Why don't you write to God, Oscar?"

"Oh no, not you, Mamie-Rose!"

"What do you mean, not me?"

"Not you! I didn't think you'd be a liar."

"But I'm not lying to you."

"Then why talk to me about God? They've already pulled the Santa Claus one on me. Once is enough!"

"Oscar, there is no earthly connection between God and Santa Claus."

"Oh yes, there is. Same thing. Brainwashing and so on!"

"Do you really suppose that I, a former wrestler, who won a hundred and sixty matches out of a hundred and sixty-five, forty-three of them KO, the Strangler of Languedoc, could believe in Santa Claus for one second?"

"No."

"Well then, I don't believe in Santa Claus but I do believe in God. So there."

Obviously, put that way it changed everything.

"And why should I write to God?"

"You'd feel less alone."

"Less alone with someone who doesn't exist?"

"Make him exist."

She leaned over to me.

"Each time that you believe in him, he'll exist a little bit more. If you persist, he'll exist completely. And then he can do you some good."

"What should I write him?"

"Whatever you're thinking. Thoughts you don't tell to anyone are thoughts that weigh heavily, get stuck, make you more tense, immobilize you, take the place of new ideas and then putrefy you. You'll become a dump for old thoughts that will stink if you don't speak up."

"OK."

"And besides, you can ask one thing a day of God. Careful, though! Just one thing."

"He's useless, your God, Mamie-Rose. Aladdin had the right to three wishes with the genie in the lamp."

"One wish a day is better than three in a lifetime, no?"

"OK. So I can order anything from him? Toys, candy, a car . . ."

"No, Oscar. God is not Santa Claus. You can only ask for things of the spirit."

"Such as?"

"Such as courage, patience, explanations."

"OK, I see."

"And what you can also do, Oscar, is suggest to him he do certain favors for others."

"One wish a day, Mamie-Rose. Come off it, I'll start by keeping it for myself!"

There it is. So, God, on the occasion of this first letter I've shown you a little of what my life in the hospital is like here, where they now see me as an obstacle to medicine, and I'd like to ask you for clarification on one point: Am I going to get better? Just answer yes or no. It's not very complicated. Yes or no. All you have to do is cross out the wrong answer.

More tomorrow, kisses,

Oscar

P.S. I don't have your address: What do I do?

Dear God,

Bravo! You're really something. Even before I mailed the letter you gave me the answer. How'd you do that?

This morning I was playing chess with Einstein in the recreation room when Popcorn came to warn me:

"Your parents are here."

"My parents? Impossible. They only come on Sundays."

"I saw the car. A red Jeep with a white canvas roof."

"Impossible."

I shrugged my shoulders and went on playing with Einstein. But since I was very distracted, Einstein took all my pieces and that irritated me even more. If we call him Einstein, it's not because he's more intelligent than the rest of us but because his head is twice as big. It seems there's water inside his. It's a pity. If it was all brains, he'd be able to do great things, Einstein could.

When I saw that I was going to lose, I stopped playing and followed Popcorn, whose room looks out over the parking lot. He was right: my parents were there.

I should tell you, God, that we live far away, my parents and I. I wasn't aware of that when I lived there but now that I don't live there any more, I really think it's very far away. As a result, my parents can only come to see me once a week, on Sundays, because they don't work on Sundays, and neither do I.

"You see, I told you so," Popcorn said. "What'll you give me for having clued you in?"

"I have chocolate with nuts."

"No more Tagada strawberries?"

"No."

"OK, chocolate then."

Obviously, we're not supposed to give any food to Popcorn since he is here to lose weight. Two hundred and fifteen pounds when you're nine years old and three and a half feet tall by three and a half feet wide! The only piece of clothing he can get his entire body into is a striped American sweatshirt. And even then, the stripes are seasick. Frankly, since none of my buddies or I believe he'll ever be able to stop being fat and we feel so sorry for how hungry he is all the time, we always give him our leftovers. One chocolate is minuscule compared to such a heap of fat! If this is wrong for us to do, then the nurses, too, should stop shoving suppositories in him.

I went back to my room to wait for my parents. At first I didn't notice the minutes go by because I was out of breath. Then I realized that they could have come to me fifteen times over.

Suddenly I figured out where they were. I slipped into the hallway; when nobody saw me, I went down the staircase and walked to Dr. Düsseldorf's office in the semi-dark.

I knew it! There they were. I could hear the voices behind the door. Since I was exhausted from coming down the stairs, I took a few seconds to let my heart find its proper place and that's when everything unraveled. I heard what I shouldn't have heard. My mother was sobbing, and Dr. Düsseldorf kept repeating, "We've tried everything. Please believe me when I say that we've tried everything," and in a strained voice my father kept answering, "I'm sure you have, Doctor, I'm sure of that."

I stayed there with my ear glued to the metal door. I didn't know any longer what was coldest, the metal or me.

Dr. Düsseldorf said:

"Would you like to go and give him a hug?"

"I would never have the courage," my mother said.

"He shouldn't see us in this state," my father added.

And that's when I knew my parents were both cowards. Worse: two cowards who were taking me for a coward!

When I heard the noise of chairs moving in the office, I guessed they were leaving and I opened the first door I saw.

That's how I found myself in the broom closet where I spent the rest of the morning since, and maybe you don't know this, God, broom closets open from the outside but not from the inside, as if people were afraid that at night the brooms, buckets, and mops might walk out!

In any event, it didn't bother me to be locked up in the dark because I really didn't feel like seeing anybody any more and because my arms and legs weren't terribly responsive either after the shock I had when I heard what I had heard.

Toward noon, I sensed there was a lot of commotion on the floor above me. I was listening to footsteps and then a stampede. Then they started to call out my name from every direction:

"Oscar! Oscar!"

It really did me a load of good to hear them call me and not to answer. I felt like annoying the entire world.

Soon afterward I think I must have slept a little and then I noticed the sound of Madame N'da's dragging feet in her clogs—she is the cleaning lady. She opened the door and then we really scared each other and screamed really loud, she because she wasn't expecting to find me there in the closet, and I because I didn't remember her being so black. Nor her screaming so loud.

Afterward, it turned into a wild free-for-all. They all came running, Dr. Düsseldorf, the head nurse, the floor nurses, and the other housekeepers. And while I thought they were going to yell at me, they were all sniveling and I knew I should quickly take advantage of the situation.

"I want to see Mamie-Rose."

"But where did you go, Oscar? How are you feeling?"

"I want to see Mamie-Rose."

"How did you get into the closet? Did you follow someone? Did you hear something?"

"I want to see Mamie-Rose."

"Have a glass of water."

"No. I want to see Mamie-Rose."

"Have a bit of . . ."

"No. I want to see Mamie-Rose."

Granite. A cliff. A cement slab. Nothing to be done. I wasn't even listening to what they were saying to me any more. I wanted to see Mamie-Rose.

Dr. Düsseldorf looked very frustrated not to have any authority over me whatsoever in front of his colleagues. He ended up by giving in.

"Someone go and find that lady!"

Then I agreed to rest in my room and I slept a little. When I woke up, Mamie-Rose was there. She was smiling.

"Bravo, Oscar, that did the trick. You certainly hit them hard. But the result is that they're jealous of me now."

"I don't care."

"They're decent people, Oscar. Very decent people."

"I don't give a damn."

"What's wrong?"

"Dr. Düsseldorf told my parents I'm going to die and they ran off. I hate them."

I told her everything in great detail, as I'm telling you now, God.

"Hmmm," Mamie-Rose went, "that reminds me of my match in Bethune against Sarah Youp La Boom, the wrestler with the oiled body, the eel of the ring, an acrobat who'd fight almost naked and slither through your fingers when you tried to get a hold on her. She only fought in Bethune where she'd win the Cup of Bethune every single year. And I really begrudged her that Cup of Bethune!"

"What did you do, Mamie-Rose?"

"Friends of mine threw some flour when she climbed into the ring. Oil and flour make very nice bread crumbs.

I had her down on the mat in five movements, that Sarah Youp La Boom. After me, they no longer called her the eel of the ring but the breaded cod."

"You'll pardon me, Mamie-Rose, but I don't really get the connection."

"It's very clear to me, though. There's always a solution, Oscar. There's always a bag filled with flour somewhere. You should write to God. He's stronger than I."

"Even in wrestling?"

"Yes. Even in wrestling, God knows a thing or two. Try it, my little Oscar. What hurts you the most?"

"I hate my parents."

"So then go ahead and really hate them very much."

"Mamie-Rose, is that you telling me that?"

"Yes. Hate them very much. That will keep you busy. And when you're done fretting, you'll see it wasn't worth it. Tell all that to God and ask him in your letter to pay you a visit."

"He moves around?"

"In his own way. Not often. Very rarely, in fact."

"Why? Is he sick, too?"

From Mamie-Rose's sigh I understood then that she didn't want to admit to me that you, God, are also not in good shape.

"Didn't your parents ever speak to you about God, Oscar?"

"Just drop it. My parents are stupid."

"Of course. But didn't they ever speak to you about God?"

"Yes, but only once. To tell me they didn't believe in him. They only believe in Santa Claus."

"Are they that stupid, my little friend?"

"You can't even imagine! The day I came home from school and told them that they should stop making a fool out of me, that I knew like all my buddies that Santa Claus didn't exist, they looked like they'd just fallen from the sky. Since I was pretty furious about having seemed like a moron in the school yard, they swore to me they'd never meant to deceive me and that they, too, had honestly believed Santa Claus existed and they were terribly disappointed to learn it wasn't true! Two real freaks, I'm telling you, Mamie-Rose!"

"So they don't believe in God?"

"No."

"And that didn't puzzle you?"

"If I were interested in what idiots think, I wouldn't have any time left for what intelligent people think."

"You're right, there. But the fact that your parents who, according to you, are idiots . . ."

"Yes. Real idiots, Mamie-Rose!"

"So, if your parents who make mistakes don't believe in him, then is that in itself not enough reason for you to believe in him and ask him to pay you a visit?"

"True. But didn't you tell me he was bedridden?"

"No. He has a very special way of coming to visit. He comes and visits you in your thoughts. In your mind."

That really appealed to me. I thought that was really very neat. Mamie-Rose added:

"You'll see, his visits help a lot."

"OK, I'll talk to him about it. Anyway, for the moment, the visits that help me the most are your visits."

Mamie-Rose smiled and bent over almost shyly to kiss me on the cheek. She didn't dare really do it. She was asking me for permission with the look in her eyes.

"Go ahead. Give me a kiss. I won't tell the others. I wouldn't want to ruin your reputation as a former wrestler."

Her lips were on my cheeks and that really pleased me. It gave me a warm feeling and made me tingle, it smelled of powder and soap.

"When are you coming back?"

"I'm only allowed to come twice a week."

"Now that's not possible, Mamie-Rose! I'm not going to wait for three whole days!"

"That's the rule."

"Who makes those rules?"

"Dr. Düsseldorf."

"Right now Dr. Düsseldorf pees in his pants when he sees me. Go and ask his permission, Mamie-Rose. I'm not kidding."

She looks at me and hesitates.

"I'm not kidding. If you don't come to see me every day I'm not going to write to God."

"I'll try."

Mamie-Rose left the room and I started to cry.

I didn't realize before how much I needed help. I didn't realize before how truly sick I was. The idea of not seeing Mamie-Rose any more made me understand that, and here I was, tears streaming down and burning my cheeks.

Fortunately, I had a bit of time to pull myself together before she came back in.

"It's all set. I have his permission. For the next twelve days I'm allowed to come and see you every day."

"Me, and only me?"

"You, and only you, Oscar. Twelve days."

And then I don't know what came over me but the tears started again and I was shaking. And yet, I know boys aren't supposed to cry, especially me who, with my bald head, doesn't look like either a boy or a girl but more like a Martian. Nothing to be done about that. I just couldn't stop.

"Twelve days? I'm doing that bad, Mamie-Rose?"

She, too, was sorely tempted to start crying. She hesitated. The former wrestler kept the former girl from letting go. It was sweet to watch and distracted me a little.

"What day is this, Oscar?"

"What a question! There's my calendar. It's the 19th of December."

"In the region where I come from, Oscar, there is a legend that claims that for the last twelve days of the year you may guess at what the weather will be like in the twelve months to come. All you have to do is watch each day to know what the month of the following year looks like. The 19th of December is the month of January, the 20th is February, and so on, until December 31st, which foreshadows the month of December of next year."

"Is it true?"

"It's a legend. The legend of the twelve divinatory days. I would like the two of us to play this game, you and I. Well, you especially. Starting today, you'll keep a close watch on every day and tell yourself that each day counts for ten years."

"Ten years?"

"Yes. One day: ten years."

"So in twelve days, I'll be a hundred and thirty!"

"Yes. Can you imagine?"

Mamie-Rose kissed me—I can tell she's enjoying this—and then left.

So here we go, God: I was born this morning and wasn't really aware of it; it became more obvious by noon when I was five, I gained awareness but it wasn't to get any good news; this evening, I am ten and that's the age of reason. I'll make use of that by asking you one thing: when you have something to tell me as you did at noon when I was five years old, do it a little less roughly. Thanks.

More tomorrow, kisses,

Oscar

P.S. I have something to ask you. I know I only have the right to one wish but my wish from just before is barely a wish, more like of a piece of advice.

I'd rather like a little visit. A little visit in spirit. I think that's so neat. I'd really like it if you'd come by. My hours are from eight in the morning until nine at night. The rest of the time I'm asleep. Even during the day I catch a little snooze sometimes because of the treatments. But if you find me napping, don't hesitate to wake me up. It would be really dumb to miss each other by a minute, don't you think?

Dear God,

Today I experienced my adolescence and it was not exactly a smooth ride. What a story! I had lots of problems with my friends and my parents, and all that because of girls. I'm not unhappy this evening, now that I am twenty, because I'm telling myself that, phew, the worst is behind me. Puberty, thanks a lot! Once is enough!

First off, God, let me remind you that you didn't come. In view of the problems of adolescence I was having today, I slept very little so I couldn't have missed you. And besides, let me say it again, if I'm dozing just shake me awake.

When I woke up, Mamie-Rose was already here. During breakfast she told me about her fights against Royal Tit, a Belgian wrestler, who'd gobble up six pounds of raw meat a day which she'd wash down with a barrel of beer; it seems that her—Royal Tit's—greatest strength was her breath because of the meat–beer fermentation, and that is what used to send her adversaries right down to the mat. In order to conquer her, Mamie-Rose had to improvise a new strategy: she put a hood infused with lavender over her head and called herself the Executioner of Carpentras. She always says that wrestling is as much a question of brains as of muscles.

"Who do you really like, Oscar?"

"Here? At the hospital?"

"Yes."

"Bacon, Einstein, Popcorn."

"And of the girls?"

That question really stopped me short. I didn't feel like answering. But Mamie-Rose was waiting and, faced with a wrestler of international fame, you can't play the fool too long.

"Peggy Blue."

Peggy Blue is the blue child. She lives in the next to the last room at the end of the hallway. She has a sweet smile but hardly ever talks. She looks like an elf that's just resting at the hospital for a moment. She has a complicated illness, the blue disease, a problem with blood that should go to the lungs but doesn't and consequently makes the whole skin bluish. She's waiting for an operation that will make her pink. I think it's a pity, I think she's very pretty in blue, Peggy Blue is. There's a lot of light and silence around her, and when she comes close you think you're going into a chapel.

"Have you told her so?"

"I'm not going to get right in her face and tell her 'Peggy Blue, I really like you.'"

"Sure. Why not?"

"I don't even know if she knows I exist."

"All the more reason."

"Have you seen what I look like? She'd really have to be fond of extraterrestrials and I'm not sure she is."

"I think you're very handsome, Oscar."

With that she put a bit of a brake on the conversation, Mamie-Rose did. It's really nice to hear things like that, it makes your skin quiver, but you don't know what to say anymore.

"I don't want to seduce her only with my looks, Mamie-Rose."

"What do you feel for her?"

"I want to protect her from ghosts."

"What? Are there ghosts here?"

"Yes. Every night. They wake us up but we don't know why. They pinch us and hurt us. We're afraid because we don't see them. Then it's hard to go back to sleep again."

"And you, do you see them often, these ghosts?"

"No. I sleep very soundly. But Peggy Blue, I hear her screaming sometimes in the middle of the night. I'd really like to protect her."

"Go and tell her."

"In any case, I couldn't really do it because we're not allowed to leave our room at night. That's the rule."

"Do ghosts know the rules? No. Of course not. Be clever: if they hear you telling Peggy Blue that you'll stand guard for her to protect her from them, they won't dare come tonight."

"But . . . but . . ."

"How old are you, Oscar?"

"I don't know. What time is it?"

"Ten o'clock. You're going on fifteen. Don't you think it's about time to have the courage of your convictions?"

At ten thirty I made up my mind and walked to the door of her room, which was open.

"Hi, Peggy. It's Oscar."

She was on her bed. You'd have thought she was Snow White waiting for the prince when those stupid dwarfs think she's dead, Snow White like in photos of snow in which the snow is blue and not white.

She turned to me and then I was wondering whether she was going to take me for the prince or one of those dwarfs. I would have checked "dwarf" because of my bald head but she said nothing, and that's what's so good about Peggy, she never says anything and everything remains a mystery.

"I've come to tell you that tonight, and every night from now on if you want me to, I'll stand watch in front of your room to protect you from the ghosts."

She looked at me, batted her eyelashes, and I had the feeling I was seeing a movie in slow motion, the air becoming more aerial, the silence more silent, me walking in water, and everything changed when you approached her bed, lit up by a light that came from nowhere.

"Hey, just a minute there, Bald Egg, I'm the one who'll watch out for Peggy!"

Popcorn was standing in the doorway or, rather, filling the doorframe. I trembled. For sure, if he stands watch it would be quite effective, no ghost could get through.

Popcorn winked at Peggy.

"Hey, Peggy? You and I, we're buddies, aren't we?"

Peggy looked at the ceiling. Popcorn took that as a confirmation and pulled me outside.

"If you want a girl, take Sandrine. Peggy is private domain."

"Says who?"

"Say I, since I got there before you. If you're not happy about that, we could have a fight."

"Actually, I'm super-happy."

I was a little tired and went to sit down in the game room. It so happened that Sandrine was there. Sandrine has leukemia, like me, but in her case it looks as if the treatment worked. We call her Chinese Girl, because she has a shiny black wig of very straight hair with bangs and that makes her look Chinese. She looks at me and pops a bubble of her bubble gum.

"You may kiss me, if you want."

"Why? Your chewing gum isn't enough for you?"

"You're not even up to it, you little nothing. I'm sure you've never even done it."

"Don't make me laugh. At fifteen I have, quite a few times already, believe me."

"You're fifteen?" she asks me, surprised.

I check my watch.

"Yeah. More than that."

"I've always dreamed of being kissed by someone older, a fifteen-year-old."

"It's tempting, that's for sure," I say.

And then she makes an impossible grimace with her lips pushed way out, you'd almost think she was a sucker getting squashed on a windowpane, and I figure she is waiting to be kissed.

As I turn around, I see all the guys watching. No way to fizzle out now. Got to be a man. It's time.

I move closer and kiss her. She grabs me with her arms, I can't get away from her, it's wet, and suddenly without warning me she passes me her chewing gum. In my surprise I swallowed the whole thing. I was furious.

At that very moment there's a hand tapping my back. Misfortune never comes alone: my parents. It was Sunday and I'd forgotten that!

"Are you going to introduce your little friend to us, Oscar?"

"She's not my friend."

"Will you introduce her anyway?"

"Sandrine. My parents. Sandrine."

"I'm delighted to meet you," says the Chinese Girl, putting on a very sweet act.

I could have strangled her.

"Would you like Sandrine to come to your room with us?"

"No. Sandrine stays here."

Back in my bed, I realized I was tired and I slept a little. In any case, I didn't want to talk to them.

When I woke up, they had obviously brought me presents. Since I've been in the hospital for good, my parents have a hard time keeping a conversation going, so they bring me presents and we spend disgusting afternoons reading game rules and instruction leaflets. My father is a staunch reader of rules—even when they're in Turkish or Japanese, it doesn't discourage him, he hangs on to the diagram. He is world champion of the ruined Sunday afternoon.

Today he brought me a CD player. I couldn't criticize that even if I'd felt like it.

"You didn't come yesterday?"

"Yesterday? Why would you think that? We can only make it on Sundays. What makes you say that?"

"Someone saw your car in the parking lot."

"Ours is not the only red Jeep in the world. Cars are interchangeable."

"Yeah. Not like parents. Pity."

With that I had them nailed to the ground. So I took the CD player and while they were there I listened to *The Nutcracker* twice, without stopping. For two hours they couldn't say a word. Just too bad for them.

"Do you like it?"

"Yeah. I'm sleepy."

They understood they had to go. They were terribly ill at ease. They couldn't decide. I sensed they wanted to say things to me and weren't able to. It felt good to see them suffer for a change.

Then my mother rushed over to me, hugged me very tightly, too tightly, and said in a shaking voice:

"I love you, my little Oscar. I love you so much."

I felt like resisting but at the last moment I let her carry on, it reminded me of before, the time when we simply used to cuddle a lot, the time when her voice wasn't all anxious when she told me she loved me.

After that I must have fallen asleep for a while.

Mamie-Rose is a master at awakening. She always gets to the finish line the moment I open my eyes. And at that very same moment she always smiles.

"So, how were your parents?"

"Zero, as always. Well, they did give me *The Nut-cracker*."

"*The Nutcracker*? That's funny. I had a friend who had that name. A real champion. She broke her adversaries' necks between her thighs. And Peggy Blue, did you go see her?"

"Don't even talk about it. She is Popcorn's fiancée."

"Is that what she told you?"

"No. He did."

"Pure bluff!"

"Don't think so. I'm sure she likes him better than me. He's stronger, more reassuring."

"Bluffing, I tell you! I looked like a mouse in the ring, and yet I beat wrestlers who looked like a whale or a hippopotamus. Look, there was Plum Pudding, the Irish woman, three hundred pounds in her underwear before she had her Guinness, forearms like my thighs, biceps like hams, legs I couldn't even get around. No waist, no holds. Unbeatable!"

"How'd you manage?"

"When there is no hold it means they're round and roll around. I made her run, to wear her out, and then I pushed her over, old Plum Pudding. They needed a winch to raise her. You, my little Oscar, have a light bone structure and not much meat on you, that's for sure, but seduction doesn't have to do with bones and meat, it has more to do with the heart. And heart you have plenty of."

"Me?"

"Go and see Peggy Blue and tell her what's in your heart."

"I'm a bit tired."

"Tired? How old are you now? Eighteen? Nobody is tired at eighteen."

Mamie-Rose really has a way with words that gives you energy.

Night came, sounds resonated more loudly in the half-dark, and the moon was reflected in the hallway linoleum.

I went into Peggy's room and held out my CD player to her.

"Here. Listen to this, the 'Waltz of the Snowflakes.' It's so pretty, it makes me think of you."

Peggy listened to the 'Waltz of the Snowflakes.' She was smiling as if it were an old friend, this waltz, telling her funny things in her ear.

She gave me back the player and said:

"That's beautiful."

It was her first word. Neat for a first word, isn't it?

"Peggy Blue, I wanted to tell you something—I don't want you to have your operation. You are beautiful like this. You are pretty in blue."

I could tell this really pleased her. That's not why I said it, but it was obvious that it pleased her.

"I want it to be you, Oscar, who protects me from the ghosts."

"Count on me, Peggy."

I was terribly proud. In the end, it was I who'd won!

"Kiss me."

Now kissing, that's really a girl's thing, almost like a need they have. But as opposed to the Chinese Girl, Peggy isn't malicious, she held out her cheek to me and, it's true, kissing her made me all warm as well.

"Goodnight, Peggy."

"Goodnight, Oscar."

That's it, God, that was my day. I gather they call adolescence the disagreeable age. It's tough. But in the end, when you get to the age of twenty, it begins to straighten out. So now I'm sending you my request of the day: I'd like for Peggy and me to be married. I'm not sure that marriage belongs to the things of the spirit, which is your domain. Do you grant that kind of wish, the wish to have a wedding performed? If that's not your department, tell me soon so that I can turn to the right person. Without meaning to rush you, I need to tell you that I don't have much time. So: marriage of Oscar and Peggy Blue. Yes or no? See if you can deal with that, it would please me very much.

More tomorrow, kisses,

Oscar

P.S. By the way, so where do you really live?

Dear God,

It's all done. I'm married. It is the 21st of December. I'm heading toward my thirtieth year and I got married. As for any children, Peggy Blue and I decided that we'll see about that later on. In fact, I think she's not ready yet.

It happened last night.

Around one in the morning I heard Peggy Blue's lament. It made me sit right up in bed. The ghosts! Peggy Blue was tormented by the ghosts and I had promised her to keep watch. She was going to realize that I was a deadbeat. She'd never say another word to me, and she'd be right.

I got up and walked right to the howling sounds. When I came to Peggy's room I saw her sitting in her bed, watching me arrive, and she was surprised. Me, too. I must have looked astonished, for suddenly there was Peggy Blue in front of me staring at me, mouth closed, and yet I kept hearing the cries.

So then I went on to the next door and figured out that it was Bacon who was squirming in his bed because of his burns. For one moment, that gave me a bad conscience. I thought again of the day when I set the house, the cat, the dog on fire, and even roasted the goldfish— well, I guess they must have boiled probably—and I was thinking of what they must have suffered and then I said to myself that it was, after all, perhaps not so bad they died than never to be done with the memories and the burns, like Bacon, in spite of the grafts and ointments.

Bacon curled up again and stopped moaning. I went back to Peggy Blue.

"So it wasn't you, Peggy? I always thought it was you crying out at night."

"And I thought it was you!"

We couldn't get over what was happening and what we were saying to each other—it turned out that in reality each of us had been thinking of the other for a long time.

Peggy Blue turned even bluer, which, for her, meant that she was very embarrassed.

"What are you doing now, Oscar?"

"And you, Peggy?"

It's crazy how many things we have in common—the same ideas, the same questions.

"Do you want to sleep with me?"

Girls, they're just incredible. If it had been me, I would've spent hours, weeks, months maybe, chewing on a sentence like that in my head before saying it out loud. But she, she just comes out with it quite naturally, quite simply.

"OK."

And I climbed into bed with her. It was a little tight but the night we spent was fantastic. Peggy Blue smells of hazelnut and she has very soft skin like mine on the inside of my arms, but hers is soft all over. We slept a lot, dreamed a lot, staying together, and telling our lives to each other.

Of course, in the morning when Madame Gommette, the head nurse, found us together there was hell to pay. She started to scream, the night nurse started to scream as well, they yelled at each other, then at Peggy, then at me, doors were slamming, they called others in as witnesses, they called us "miserable little things" while we were actually very happy, and it took Mamie-Rose's arrival for the chaos to come to an end.

"Are you going to leave these kids in peace? Who is it you need to please, the patients or the rules? I don't give a damn about your rules, you can shove it. Now, silence! Go fight somewhere else. Just get off it!"

As always with Mamie-Rose, there was no comeback. She took me back to my room and I slept for a while.

We talked when I woke up.

"So, Oscar, it's serious then, with Peggy?"

"Solid as cement, Mamie-Rose. I am super-happy. We got married last night."

"Married?"

"Yes. We did everything that a man and a woman who are married do."

"Really?"

"Who do you take me for? I'm—what time is it?—I'm more than twenty, I'm going to run my life the way I see fit, no?"

"Sure."

"And just imagine, all those things I thought were disgusting before, when I was young, kisses and caresses, well, in the end it was really good. It's funny how we change, isn't it?"

"I'm thrilled for you, Oscar. You're growing up nicely."

"There's just one thing we didn't do, the kiss where your tongues come together. Peggy Blue was afraid it would make her have children. What do you think about that?"

"I think she's right."

"Oh really? You can have children if you kiss each other on the mouth? Well, then I'm going to have one with the Chinese Girl."

"Take it easy, Oscar. The chances are very small. Very small, indeed."

She looked very sure of what she said, Mamie-Rose did, and that calmed me down a little because, I have to tell you, God, and only you, with Peggy Blue we did put our tongues together once, well actually twice, or maybe more.

I slept some. Then we had lunch together, Mamie-Rose and I, and I began to do better.

"It's crazy how tired I was this morning."

"That's normal. Between twenty and twenty-five you go out at night, you party, you lead a wild life, and you don't spare yourself enough. You pay the price. What if we went to see God?"

"Ah, there we are, you have his address?"

"I think he's in the chapel."

Mamie-Rose dressed me as if we were going off to the North Pole, she took me in her arms and brought me to the chapel at the back of the hospital garden, beyond the frozen lawns, well, I won't explain to you where it is, since it's where you live.

It did give me a shock when I saw your statue, what I mean is when I saw the state you were in, almost all naked and very skinny there on your cross with wounds everywhere, your skull bleeding beneath the thorns, and your head not even up on your neck any more. It made me think of myself. I thought it was horrendous. Me, if I were God, like you, I would not have let them treat me that way.

"Mamie-Rose, let's be serious: you who are a wrestler, you who were a great champion, you're not really going to put your trust in that!"

"Why Oscar? Would you give God more credit if you saw a body-builder with well-worked beef, bulging muscles, oiled skin, short haircut, and tiny shorts that show everything off?"

"Well . . ."

"Think, Oscar. What do you feel closest to? A God who feels nothing or a God who suffers?"

"The one who suffers, obviously. But if I were he, if I were God, if I had the means as he does, I would have avoided any pain."

"No one can avoid pain. Not God, not you. Not your parents, not I."

"OK, fine. But why should we suffer?"

"Exactly. There's pain and there's pain. Look at his face again. Take a good look. Does he seem to be suffering?"

"No. It's odd. He doesn't look like he's in pain."

"See. You have to distinguish between two kinds of suffering, my little Oscar, physical pain and mental pain. Physical pain is what happens to you. Mental pain is what you choose."

"I don't understand."

"If they drive nails into your wrists or feet, obviously you will be in pain. You submit to it. On the other hand, you don't have to be in pain at the idea of dying. You really don't know what it is. And so it depends on you."

"Do *you* know anyone who's thrilled at the idea of dying?"

"Yes, I do. My mother was that way. On her deathbed she was smiling with eagerness, she was impatient, she was in a hurry to discover what was going to happen."

I couldn't argue anymore and, since I was anxious to hear the rest, I let a little time go by while I was contemplating what she had told me.

"But most people have no curiosity. They clutch on to what they have, like a louse in a bald man's ear. Take my Irish rival, Plum Pudding, for example, three hundred pounds on an empty stomach and in her underwear, just before her Guinness. She'd always say to me, 'Sorry about that, but me, I won't die; I don't agree and I haven't signed on.' But she was wrong. No one had told her that life was supposed to be eternal, no one! She just stubbornly believed it, rebelled, refused the whole idea of passing, she went mad, got depressed, lost weight, and then she stopped fighting and weighed no more than seventy pounds, she looked like a fishbone, and then fell apart.

You see, she died anyway, just like everybody else, but the idea of dying ruined her life."

"She was stupid, Plum Pudding was, Mamie-Rose."

"As stupid as a country sausage. But country sausage is very widely used. Very common."

There, too, I nodded my assent, because I pretty much agreed with her.

"People are afraid to die because they dread the unknown. But that's just it. What is the unknown? I recommend not being afraid but to be trusting, Oscar. Look at the face of God there on the cross—he is suffering physical pain but he does not feel any moral pain because he trusts. And so the nails hurt less. He keeps repeating to himself, 'It hurts but it cannot be an evil.' And there you have it! That is exactly the benefit of faith. I wanted to show that to you."

"OK, Mamie-Rose, when I'm scared stiff I'll force myself to have some trust."

She kissed me. In the end, we were at ease in that deserted church with you, God, who looked so at peace.

When we returned, I slept for a long time. I get more and more sleepy all the time. As if I were ravenous for it. . . . When I woke up, I said to Mamie-Rose:

"Actually, I'm not afraid of the unknown. It just bothers me to lose what I do know."

"I'm like you, Oscar. How about we invite Peggy Blue to come and have tea with us?"

Peggy Blue had tea with us; she was getting along really well with Mamie-Rose. We laughed a lot when

Mamie-Rose told us the story about her fight with the Sisters Giclette. They were triplets who pretended to be just one person. After every round, the Giclette who had worn out her adversary by prancing around, coming at her from every direction, would leap out of the ring claiming she needed to pee, she'd rush off to the bathroom and then her sister, who was in fine shape, would come back for the next round. Everybody believed there was just one Giclette and that she could bounce around without ever getting tired. Mamie-Rose discovered the trick, locked the two replacements in the bathroom, threw the key out of the window and defeated the remaining one. As a sport, wrestling is pretty cool.

Then Mamie-Rose left. The nurses are watching us, Peggy Blue and me, as if we were firecrackers about to explode. Shit, I'm thirty years old, after all! Peggy Blue swore to me that this evening she'd come to me as soon as she can manage it; in turn, I swore to her that I wouldn't put my tongue in this time.

Having children isn't all there is to it. You also need to have the time to raise them.

That's it, God. I don't know what to ask you for this evening because it was a really fine day. Oh yes, I do. Make Peggy Blue's operation tomorrow go well. Not like mine, if you see what I mean.

More tomorrow, kisses,

Oscar

P.S. Surgery is not something of the spirit. Perhaps you don't have that in store. Well, then make Peggy Blue react well to it, whatever the outcome of the operation may be. I'm counting on you.

Dear God,

Peggy Blue was operated on today. I went through ten terrible years. The thirties are difficult, it's the age of worries and responsibilities.

In fact, Peggy couldn't join me last night because Madame Ducru, the night nurse, stayed in her room to get her ready for anesthesia. The stretcher took her away around eight o'clock. It wrenched my heart when I saw Peggy Blue pass by on the rolling bed, you could hardly see her under the green sheets, she was so tiny and thin.

Mamie-Rose held my hand to keep me from getting all worked up.

"Mamie-Rose, why does God allow these things to happen to us, Peggy and me?"

"It's a good thing he makes people like you, my little Oscar, because life would be less beautiful without you."

"No. You don't understand. Why does God allow people to be sick? Either he's just mean or he's not really all that great."

"Sickness, Oscar, is like death. It's a fact. It's not a punishment."

"I can tell you're not sick!"

"And what would you know about that, Oscar?"

That stopped me short. I never dreamed Mamie-Rose, who is always so available and attentive, might have her own problems, too.

"Shouldn't be keeping things from me, Mamie-Rose, you can tell me everything. I'm at least thirty-two, I have cancer, and a wife in the operating room, so really, I know what life is."

"I love you, Oscar."

"Me too. What can I do for you and your problems? Would you like me to adopt you?"

"Adopt me?"

"Yes, I already adopted Bernard when I saw that he felt blue."

"Bernard?"

"My bear. There. In the closet. On the shelf. He's my old bear, he's got no eyes any more, no mouth, no nose, lost half of his stuffing, and he has scars all over. He looks a little like you. I adopted him the night my two stupid parents brought me a new bear. As if I was going to accept having a new one! They might as well have replaced me with a completely new little brother while they were at it! So then I adopted him. I'm leaving Bernard everything I own. I want to adopt you as well, if that would make you feel better."

"Yes, I'd like that. I think it would make me feel a lot better."

"Well, it's a deal then, Mamie-Rose."

Then we went to prepare Peggy's room, put chocolates down, and brought flowers in for her return.

Then I slept. It's crazy how much I sleep right now.

Toward the end of the afternoon Mamie-Rose woke me up to tell me that Peggy Blue was back and that the operation was a success.

Together we went to see her. Her parents were by her bedside. I don't know who had forewarned them, Peggy or Mamie-Rose, but they seemed to know who I was, they treated me very respectfully, they pulled up a chair for me so I could sit between them and I could watch over my wife together with my parents-in-law.

I was glad because Peggy was still bluish. Dr. Düsseldorf came by, rubbed his eyebrows, and said that it would begin to change in the next few hours. I looked at Peggy's mother who isn't blue but still quite beautiful, and I told myself that, after all, Peggy, my wife, could be any color she pleased, I'd love her just the same.

Peggy opened her eyes, smiled at us, at me, at her parents, and then went back to sleep.

Her parents felt reassured, but they had to leave.

"We entrust our daughter to you," they said to me. "We know we can count on you."

Mamie-Rose stayed there with me and I waited until Peggy opened her eyes a second time, then I went to my room to rest.

As I finish this letter, I realize that in the end this has been a good day today. A family day. I've adopted Mamie-Rose, I got along really well with my parents-in-law, and I have my wife back in good health even if, by eleven o'clock, she was becoming pink.

More tomorrow, kisses

Oscar

P.S. No wish today. That will give you a rest.

Dear God,

Today I went from forty to fifty and I did nothing but stupid things.

I'll tell it to you quickly because it deserves no more than that. Peggy Blue is doing fine but the Chinese Girl, sent by Popcorn who can't stand me anymore, tattled on me and told her I'd kissed her on the mouth.

The result was that Peggy told me she and I were finished. I protested. I said that what the Chinese Girl and I had done was just a bit of foolishness of youth, that it was long before she came along, and that she couldn't make me pay for my past for the rest of my life.

But she persisted. She even became good friends with the Chinese Girl just to burn me up. And I heard them laughing together.

Consequently, when Brigitte, who has Down's syndrome and always clings to everyone because that's normal with Down's syndrome people, they're just affectionate, when she came to say hi to me in my room, I let her kiss me everywhere. She was mad with joy that I allowed her to do that. You would have thought she was a dog welcoming her master. The problem was that Einstein was in the hallway. He may have water in his head but he doesn't have curtains over his eyes. He saw it all and went to tell Peggy and the Chinese Girl. Now the whole floor is treating me like a skirt chaser even though I didn't budge from my room.

"I don't know what came over me, Mamie-Rose, with Brigitte . . ."

"Midlife crisis, Oscar. Men are like that between forty-five and fifty, they need reassurance, they check to see if they're still attractive to women other than the one they love."

"That's fine, so I'm normal. But I'm pretty stupid, too, don't you think?"

"Yes. And you're totally normal."

"What should I do?"

"Who do you love?"

"Peggy. Just Peggy."

"So tell her that. A young couple is frail, always being shaken up, but if it is the right partner you just have to fight to keep it going."

Tomorrow, God, it's Christmas. I never realized that was your birthday. Make it happen that Peggy and I will be reconciled because I don't know if that's the reason why but I'm very sad this evening and have no courage left any more.

More tomorrow, kisses,

Oscar

P.S. Now that we're friends, what would you like me to get you for your birthday?

Dear God,

At eight o'clock this morning I told Peggy Blue that I loved her, only her, and that I couldn't imagine my life without her. She began to cry. She confessed that I was easing her from enormous distress because she, too, loved only me and wouldn't ever be able to find anyone else, especially now that she was pink.

It was strange, but we both began to sob, and yet it was very nice. Life as a couple is really great. Particularly after the age of fifty, when you've been through some real ordeals.

At ten o'clock I realized that it really was Christmas, that I wouldn't be able to stay with Peggy because her family—brothers, uncles, nephews, cousins—was going to land in her room and I was going to be obliged to bear up under my parents' presence. What were they going to give me this time? A puzzle consisting of eighteen thousand pieces? Books in Kurdish? A box filled with instruction leaflets? My portrait from the time when I was healthy? With two such morons, who have the brains of a garbage bag, there was a threat on the horizon. I could expect almost anything awful. The only thing I could be sure of was that it was going to be a totally stupid day.

I made up my mind very quickly and organized my escape. A little barter: my toys to Einstein, my down quilt to Bacon, and my candy to Popcorn. A little observation: Mamie-Rose always went through the coatroom before she left. A little foresight: my parents wouldn't come before noon. Everything went quite smoothly: at eleven thirty, Mamie-Rose kissed me and wished me a nice Christmas Day with my parents, then disappeared to the floor where the coatroom is. I whistled. Popcorn, Einstein, and Bacon got me dressed very fast, supported me as they helped me downstairs and carried me right to Mamie-Rose's jalopy, a car that must date back to some time before the automobile. Popcorn, who's very talented at opening locks because he was lucky enough to have grown up in a disadvantaged neighborhood, picked the lock of the rear door and they threw me on the floor between the front and the back seats. Then they returned, sight unseen, to the building.

After quite a long time, Mamie-Rose got into her car, made it sputter ten or fifteen times before it would start up and then, at a hellish pace, we left. It's brilliant, this kind of car from before the automobile, it makes such a racket that you feel as if you're going really fast and it shakes as much as a ride at the fair.

The problem is that Mamie-Rose must have learned how to drive from a stunt man—she pays no attention to any stoplights, sidewalks, or traffic circles to the point that every now and then the car would lift right off the ground. There was quite a din inside, she honked a lot, and, where vocabulary was concerned, it was an enriching experience, as well. She let fly all kinds of terrible words with which to insult the enemies that crossed her path, and once again I told myself that wrestling certainly is a good school for life.

I'd planned to leap out of the car when we arrived and say, "Hi there, Mamie-Rose," but the obstacle course to her house took such a very long time that I must have fallen asleep.

The fact remains that when I woke up it was dark, it was cold and silent, and I was alone lying on a humid rug. That was when I thought for the first time that I had perhaps done something foolish.

I got out of the car and it began to snow. It was a whole lot less pleasant than the "Waltz of the Snowflakes" in *The Nutcracker*. My teeth were chattering.

I saw a large house all lit up. I walked. I was in pain. I must have jumped up so high just to reach the doorbell that I collapsed on the mat.

That's where Mamie-Rose found me.

"But . . . but . . . ," she started to say.

Then she bent over me and mumbled:

"My darling."

That's when I thought that perhaps what I had done wasn't so foolish.

She carried me into her living room where she had put up a big blinking Christmas tree. I was surprised to see how beautiful it was at Mamie-Rose's house. She made me warm up next to the fire and we drank a large cup of hot chocolate. I suspected that she wanted to make sure I was all right before she'd bawl me out. So, I took all the time in the world to pull myself together, which wasn't very hard to do, besides, because I'm really tired these days.

"Everyone at the hospital is looking for you, Oscar. They're sounding the alarm. Your parents are desperate. They've alerted the police."

"That doesn't surprise me from them. If they're stupid enough to think I'll love them when I'm in handcuffs . . ."

"What do you hold against them?"

"They're afraid of me. They don't dare talk to me. And the less they dare, the more I feel like a monster. Why do I scare them so? Am I that ugly? Do I stink? Have I grown into an idiot without knowing it?"

"They're not afraid of you, Oscar. They're afraid of your illness."

"My illness is a part of me. They don't have to act differently because I'm sick. Or can they only love an Oscar who's healthy?"

"They love you, Oscar. They told me so."

"You talk to them?"

"Yes. They're very jealous that we get along so well. No, not jealous. Sad. Sad that they can't manage that as well."

I shrugged my shoulders but I was already a little less mad. Mamie-Rose made me another cup of hot chocolate.

"You know, Oscar, one day you will die. But your parents, too, will die."

I was surprised by what she told me. I'd never thought of that.

"Yes. They too will die. All alone. And with the dreadful remorse of not having been able to reconcile themselves with their only child, an Oscar they adored."

"Don't say things like that, Mamie-Rose. It makes me depressed."

"Think about them, Oscar. You figured out that you are dying because you are a very smart boy. But you haven't figured out yet that you're not the only one who's dying. Everybody dies. One day your parents. One day me."

"Yes, but still I'm going first."

"That's true. You're going first. However, does that mean that just because you're going first, you have the right to do anything and everything? And the right to forget about others?"

"I get it, Mamie-Rose. Why don't you call them then."

There it is, God. I'll give you the short version of what happened next because my wrist is getting tired. Mamie-Rose informed the hospital, who informed my parents, who came to Mamie-Rose's house and we all celebrated Christmas together.

When my parents arrived, I said:

"Excuse me, but I forgot that you two are also going to die one day."

I don't know what that sentence loosened up inside them, but after that they were just the way they used to be before and we had a super Christmas evening.

With dessert Mamie-Rose wanted to watch midnight mass on television and also a wrestling match she had taped. She says that she's been doing this for years, she always keeps a wrestling match to look at to warm up before midnight mass, that it's a habit and one she really likes. So we all watched a fight she'd put aside. It was fantastic. Mephista against Joan of Arc! Bathing suits and thigh boots! Wild and strapping ladies! as Papa said, who was all red and seemed to love the wrestling. You can't imagine how many punches they put on each other's faces. I would've been dead a hundred times over in a fight like that. Mamie-Rose told me that getting punched in the face is a question of training, the more you get the more you can take. Always keep hoping. In fact, it was Joan of Arc who won, which you wouldn't have expected at first: that must have made you happy.

By the way, happy birthday, God. Mamie-Rose, who's just tucked me into the bed of her oldest son who was a veterinarian in Congo with the elephants, suggested that it was a very nice birthday present to you, my reconciliation with my parents. Frankly, I think it's not much of a present myself. But if Mamie-Rose who is an old friend of yours says so . . .

More tomorrow, kisses,

Oscar

P.S. I forgot my wish—that my parents will always be like tonight. And me, too. It was a great Christmas, especially Mephista against Joan of Arc. Sorry about the mass. I dropped off before that.

Dear God,

I am over sixty years old now and I'm paying the price for all the abuse I committed last night. I wasn't in very good shape today.

It was nice to come back to my room at the hospital. That's how it gets to be when you're old, you don't like to travel any more. I sure have no desire to leave again.

What I didn't tell you yesterday in my letter was that at Mamie-Rose's there was a statue of Peggy Blue on a shelf in the staircase. I swear it. Exactly the same, made of plaster with the same very sweet face, and her clothes and her skin the same color blue. Mamie-Rose claims it's the Virgin Mary, your mother from what I understand, a Madonna that's been in her family for several generations. She let me keep her. I put her on my bedside table. In any case, it will go back to Mamie-Rose's family one day since I've adopted her.

Peggy Blue is doing better. She came to visit me in a wheelchair. She didn't recognize herself in the statue but we had a nice time together. We listened to *The Nutcracker* holding hands and it reminded us of the good old times.

I won't talk to you much longer because the pen is a little heavy right now. Everyone here is sick, even Dr. Düsseldorf, because of all the chocolates, the foie gras, the marrons glacés, and the champagne that all the parents gave to the nursing staff. I'd really like it if you'd pay me a visit.

Kisses, more tomorrow,

Oscar

Dear God,

Today I went from seventy to eighty and it made me think a lot.

First of all, I used the present I got from Mamie-Rose for Christmas. I don't know if I told you about it? It's a plant from the Sahara that lives its whole life in a single day. As soon as the seed gets water it starts to bud, it becomes a stem, it grows leaves, it makes a flower, manufactures seeds, fades, flattens out, and just like that it's gone by the evening. It's a brilliant gift. I thank you for having invented that. We watered it at seven o'clock this morning, Mamie-Rose, my parents, and I—actually, I don't know if I mentioned it, but they're living with Mamie-Rose for now because it's less far away—and I was able to follow its whole existence. I was really moved. For sure, as a flower it's rather scrawny and way too small—it's nothing like a baobab but it did its job as a plant very nicely, just like a big plant, in front of our eyes in one day without stopping.

I spent a lot of time reading the medical dictionary with Peggy Blue. It's her favorite book. She's fascinated with diseases and wonders which ones she might have later on. I looked up the words I'm interested in: "life," "death," "faith," "God." You can believe me if you want, but they weren't there! That already proves they aren't diseases, life, death, faith, or you. Which is rather good news. Still, in such a serious book, there should be answers to the most serious questions, don't you think?

"Mamie-Rose, it seems to me that in the medical dictionary there are only special things, problems that this one or that one might have. But the things that concern us all aren't in there: life, death, faith, God."

"Perhaps you should check a dictionary of philosophy, Oscar. However, even if you were to find the ideas you're looking for, you might well be disappointed too. It offers several very different answers for each concept."

"How can that be?"

"The most interesting questions continue to be questions. They are the wrapping around a mystery. You should add 'perhaps' to every answer. Only uninteresting questions have a definite answer."

"Do you mean there's no solution for 'life'?"

"I mean that for 'life' there are several solutions, therefore no solution."

"That's what I think, too, Mamie-Rose, there's no solution to life other than living."

Dr. Düsseldorf came by to see us. He had his beaten-dog look on, which makes him even more expressive with his huge black eyebrows.

"Do you have your eyebrows done, Dr. Düsseldorf?" I asked.

He looked around, very surprised, and seemed to be asking Mamie-Rose and my parents if he'd heard it right. In a stifled voice he ended up by saying yes.

"Shouldn't make a face like that, Dr. Düsseldorf. Listen, I'm going to be very open with you because I've always been very reasonable where medication was concerned and you've been perfect where illness is concerned. Stop looking so guilty. It's not your fault that you're forced to give bad news to people, diseases with Latin names, and recuperation that won't happen. You should relax. Loosen up. You're not God the Father. You're not the one who orders nature around. You're just the repairman. You should slow down, Dr. Düsseldorf, let go a bit, and not take yourself too seriously, or else you won't be able to keep up this work for very long. Just look at that face of yours already."

As he was listening to me, Dr. Düsseldorf's mouth appeared to have swallowed an egg whole. Then he smiled, a real smile, and kissed me.

"You're absolutely right, Oscar. Thank you for telling me that."

"No problem, Doctor. My pleasure. Come back whenever you want."

That's it, God. You, on the other hand, you haven't visited me yet and I'm still waiting. Please come. Don't hesitate. Come, even if I have a lot of company these days. It would really make me happy.

More tomorrow, kisses,

Oscar

Dear God,

Peggy Blue left. She went home to her parents' house. I'm not stupid, I know I'll never see her again.

I'm not writing to you because I'm just too sad. We spent our life together, Peggy and I, and now I'm all alone in my bed, bald, soft, and tired. It's lousy to grow old.

Today I don't like you any more.

Oscar

Dear God,

Thank you for coming.

You really picked the right moment because I wasn't doing well at all. Maybe you were annoyed also because of my letter from yesterday . . .

When I woke up, I figured I was ninety years old and I turned my head toward the window to watch the snow.

And that's when I surmised you were coming. It was morning. I was all alone on Earth. It was so early that even the birds were still sleeping, even the night nurse, Madame Ducru, must have caught a quick nap, and you were busy putting the dawn together. You were having a hard time but you persisted. The sky became paler. You were inflating the air with white, gray, blue. You were pushing the night away and reviving the world. You didn't stop. That's when I understood the difference between you and us—you're the indefatigable guy! The one who never gets weary. Always working. And here's the day! And here's the night! And here's springtime! And here's winter! And here's Peggy Blue! And here's Oscar! And here's Mamie-Rose! Such fine health!

I understood that you were here. That you were telling me your secret: look at the world every day as if for the first time.

So I followed your advice and I really made an effort. The first time. I contemplated the light, colors, trees, birds, animals. I felt the air go through my nostrils and it made me breathe. I heard the voices rising in the hallway as in the vault of a cathedral. I felt alive. I was shivering with pure joy. The bliss of existing. I was enchanted.

Thank you, God, for having done that for me. I felt as if you were taking me by the hand and bringing me right into the heart of the mystery to let me contemplate that mystery. Thank you.

More tomorrow, kisses,

Oscar

P.S. My wish: Can you do this first-time thing again for my parents? Mamie-Rose knows it already, I believe. And then for Peggy, too, if you have time . . .

Dear God,

Today I am one hundred. Like Mamie-Rose. I'm sleeping a lot but I feel good.

I tried to explain to my parents that life is quite a gift. At first you overestimate it, this gift; you think you've received eternal life. Then you underestimate it, you think it stinks, it's too short, you're almost ready to throw it away. Finally, you realize that it wasn't a gift at all, just a loan. Then you try to deserve it. Me, with my one hundred years, I know what I'm talking about. The more you age, the more you have to prove you know how to savor life and appreciate it. You have to become refined, artistic. Any moron can enjoy life at the age of ten or twenty, but at a hundred when you can't move anymore, you should use your intelligence.

I don't know if I really convinced them all that well. Visit them. Finish the work. I'm getting a little tired. More tomorrow, kisses,

Oscar

Dear God,

A hundred and ten. That's really old. I think I'm beginning to die.

Oscar

Dear God,

The little boy is dead.

I will always be the lady in pink but I won't be Mamie-Rose any more. That was only for Oscar.

He died this morning during the thirty minutes that his parents and I went to get some coffee. He did it without us. I think he waited for that moment just to spare us. As if he wanted to protect us from the violence of seeing him go. Actually, it was he who was watching over us.

My heart is heavy, so heavy. Oscar lives in there and I cannot chase him out. I should keep my tears to myself for now, until tonight, because I don't want to compare my sorrow to the insurmountable grief of his parents.

Thank you for letting me know Oscar. Thanks to him, I was funny, I invented legends, I even knew something about wrestling. Thanks to him, I laughed and I knew joy. He helped me believe in you. I'm so full of love it hurts; he gave me so much of it that I have enough for all the years to come.

Until soon,

Mamie-Rose

P.S. *For the last three days, Oscar had a sign on his bedside table. I think it's meant for you. On it he had written: "Only God is allowed to wake me up."*